Pursuit of Grace

Aboard the *Empress of Ireland*

by Stephen Pavey

PublishAmerica
Baltimore

First printing

This is a work of fiction. Names, characters, places, and incidents either are the product of the author's imagination or are used fictitiously. Any resemblance to actual persons, living or dead, events, or locales is entirely coincidental

PublishAmerica has allowed this work to remain exactly as the author intended, verbatim, without editorial input.

All photos are used with permission: The Salvation Army Archives, Canada and Bermuda Territory

Front Cover artwork: Gerard Klaucke

ISBN: 1-60474-130-9
PUBLISHED BY PUBLISHAMERICA, LLLP
www.publishamerica.com
Baltimore

Printed in the United States of America

Acknowledgments

I wish to gratefully acknowledge the kind assistance of Mr. David Zeni, author of Forgotten Empress: The Empress of Ireland Story. All photos are supplied with permission of The Salvation Army Archives, Canada and Bermuda Territory, with assistance from Lieut.-Colonel John Carew. The cover design is courtesy of Gerard Klaucke, good friend of the CSB. Thank you to Dr. Roger Green for his kind words. Special thanks to Mom and Dad, Valerie, and Rhonda for all their hard work. Thanks to my family for your continued support.

Foreword

It was May of 1914. My paternal grandfather was a Canadian Salvation Army officer who was scheduled to be aboard the Canadian Pacific liner Empress of Ireland along with 200 other Salvation Army church members. They were journeying to London to attend The Salvation Army's International Congress. Circumstances prevented him from going, which at the time was a great disappointment. He could not have known at the time that 167 Salvationists would be lost, along with almost a thousand other passengers and crew, a tragedy bringing to mind the sinking of the Titanic.

This is the story of the sinking of the Empress of Ireland told as a historical novel through the life of a young woman by the name of Grace who was accompanying her father on the voyage. Here is a difficult genre to create, but Stephen Pavey does a masterful job. The character development of Grace as well as those whom she encounters in this tragic journey is well done, and no historical facts were sacrificed in the telling of this story. Likewise, because there were so many Salvationists aboard at the time, the writer places them into the story both for historical accuracy and for fictional background to the adventures of Grace aboard this doomed ship.

The author has written a story of intrigue and mystery involving Grace and others on board, and mystery lovers will find that they are moved along by the story line. Both the drama and the pathos of the story increase as the book moves along and then there is the tragic moment when many lives are changed in an instant.

Here is a historical novel worth the attention of every reader, not only because it vividly imagines the sinking of the Empress of Ireland, but also because it speaks clearly of the possibility of redemption in the midst of such tragedy. The title is well chosen—there is the pursuit of Grace in this novel, but it is Grace that exceeds the main character of the book. I am pleased to recommend this novel, and know that all who read it will be both intrigued and inspired.

Roger J. Green, Ph.D., D.D.
Professor and Chair of Biblical and Theological Studies
Terrelle B. Crum Chair of Humanities
Gordon College
Wenham, Massachusetts

"Time is the coin of your life. It is the only coin you have, and only you can determine how it will be spent. Be careful lest you let other people spend it for you."

—Carl Sandberg

Pursuit of Grace

Aboard the *Empress of Ireland*

Chapter 1

The best action is a swift action. Grace thought of these words, so often uttered from her father's lips. *Should I go along with it, or should I run?* she wondered in anticipation of the top of the gangway. It wasn't in her to go against her father's wishes. A girl of only sixteen, defying her father. It was inconceivable. She should have spoken out earlier. Much earlier.

Now steps from the top of the gangway, the water could be seen in the foreboding gap below, between the pier and the dark hull of the towering ship. Grace would forever remember today, May 28, 1914, as the day she was torn from her home—her Canada.

"Grace, could you hurry, dear? It's almost 3:30. Surely, you don't mean for us to stand here all afternoon, lest the ship pull away and we all fall into the river," spoke Harriet with an artificial laugh, but a pointed tone.

One more step and Grace would be off the gangway and into the opening of the metal hull on what appeared to be the highest deck to run all the way from the stem of the ship to the stern. Grace noticed a brass sign on the inside that read "Shelter Deck".

"We must go now, Grace. It will be alright," spoke a subtle

voice behind her that she recognized as her father's. He gently ushered her along by sliding his arm into her right arm and accompanying her through the doorway. In order to avoid a fall, she had to lift her long, narrow hobble dress slightly so that she could see her pointed boot making contact with the floor. An anxious Harriet, and her accompanying maid and chaperone, Winifred, eagerly followed.

Grace's father, Jeremiah Hathaway and his bride-to-be, Harriet Price, walked towards a ship's officer to get information on their accommodations. The brim of the crewman's hat appeared as polished as the buttons on his double-breasted tunic. His waxed moustache curled at either end, as he spoke to Mr. Hathaway who looked equally exquisite. Grace's father's bow tie sat neatly over his high collar, trimmed nicely under his three-button sack coat. His immaculate dark, shiny hair cropped out from under his black top hat, completing an air of certainty that he was the proper clientele for First Class accommodation. The officer gave Grace's father his full attention, pointing around in various directions, as though they shared a guaranteed familiarity with the ship. Both Harriet and Grace's father nodded in agreement with the officer.

Grace became privy to enough of the conversation floating her way that she understood that she and her father would be sleeping in a First Class cabin on the Upper Promenade Deck, with Harriet and Winifred only a few doors down the hall.

"Don't worry, Missy," spoke Winifred to Grace as they stepped aside from the gangway opening on the starboard side of the ship, allowing more passengers to scurry aboard. "Things have a funny way of working out. You'll see," she spoke in her thick East London accent, one that mirrored Harriet's, and that Grace had yet to get used to.

Grace wandered away from Winifred and walked further

inside without acknowledging her remark. She strutted straight through a short hallway about the width of the door she had just passed through and continued towards a staircase. *This must be the grand staircase that is always marvelled at on ships like these*, she thought. She grasped its smooth, curved dark wood rail. Her gloves slid upward on the rail, as she allowed her feet to follow like she were being led somewhere unknowingly. She made a ninety-degree right turn and eventually found herself in an open vestibule area with a tessellated floor pattern, accented by area carpets flanking the next set of oval-shaped stairs. She followed her feet to the stairs and continued upward a few steps, taking notice of the square-patterned, white moulded ceiling. It reminded her of the theatre that her father had taken her to on a visit to Toronto. She caught a glimpse of a sign reading "Lower Promenade Deck". Feeling that she should not stray too far from her father, particularly in new surroundings, she felt inclined to return below.

"Grace, are you up there?" trailed her father's voice from below.

"I am here, Father," she replied, leaning over the railing to reassure him that she was not lost.

Harriet's wide-brimmed hat began ascending the stairs towards Grace as her voice became increasingly boisterous with every step. Grace watched her uptight, twisting body climb the staircase, and was certain that her tapered waist was the result of an overburdened corset. "You mustn't wander like that, child," she scolded. "It is not proper to leave without asking."

"I'm sorry," said Grace, making eye contact with her father, but not Harriet.

"This is elegant, isn't it dear?" spoke Jeremiah Hathaway to his daughter as he joined the others on Lower Promenade Deck. "With my prior travelling aboard the Empress, I've come to know my way around quite a bit."

Grace found her body turning away from her company at that remark. Her feet began moving away from the others, towards a set of wooden double doors. She knew that her father was referring to the time several months ago when he travelled to London on business matters. There, he had met his new wife-to-be and forgotten all about his former love. Harriet had made the voyage to Canada several weeks ago, to rendezvous with her new fiancé. Her new steal.

"There she goes wandering again," interjected Harriet.

Grace ignored her remark and stepped through the heavy doors that led to the outer deck on the starboard side. She found her way across the pitch pine flooring planks to the edge of the deck, grasping the teak rail firmly with her white gloves. She looked down. The pier buildings and sheds looked like small pictures on a brochure. Taxi roofs appeared as a procession of brown and black coffins, slowly being led away from the ship, some of them powered by horse, and others with the new automobile engine.

"We must go to the Upper Promenade Deck and see to our accommodations, Grace," spoke her father with his usual expediency in such matters. "Our baggage should be there by now." He was a businessman and a clever gentleman. Swift action and practicality enabled him to secure a lucrative position with the Nipissing Mine of Cobalt, Ontario. He was charged with representing the mine internationally, and accompanied over $1,000,000 in silver bars on this trip alone. Through his contacts abroad, he hoped that his business sense would help him secure a similar position in England, making this his last association with his current employer. Marrying Harriet Price, the daughter of an affluent banker, would certainly aid his venture of financial security and a stable future abroad. With Harriet, now 33 and still unmarried, the likelihood of her finding any unattached young man was fleeting. She would have to settle for forty-year-old Jeremiah—and his daughter.

In the past, with her father frequently away on business, Grace would stay with her Aunt Nona in Toronto. She wondered now, if she would ever see her again. Her aunt became her second mother when her own mother died. Nona had only one child, Grace's cousin Andrew. He would have been sixteen by now—had he not drowned. Nona's grieving of Andrew was still fresh when her sister Sofia, Grace's mother, had died.

Nona had all the characteristics that Grace loved in her mother. She was kind and caring to anyone in need. Nona was the person who was the most encouraging to her sister when she wanted to start the Cobalt Mission. While her husband was a giant in the business community, Sofia turned her gaze on the downtrodden of society, organizing a mission that provided food and shelter—occasionally odd jobs for small pay. Just enough to make a small difference in society. Her kind ways helped shape Grace's manner of being.

Her father didn't always share her mother's passions. Often, she pressed her husband for money to finance her ventures of mercy. "You can't save them all," he would tell his wife, Sofia. In the end, he allowed her to sacrifice much of their existing fortune. But now, he had to take advantage of this opportunity with Harriet, for both himself and Grace.

Grace glanced again at her father's attire, then towards his wandering gaze, as more and more polished passengers spilled out onto the deck. It wasn't as though he was unkind. He had truly loved his wife. He supported her mission. But, now he had moved on. He was simply—on a mission of his own.

"Ladies, shall we make for our rooms and settle in, so we can be back on deck for the grand send-off?" spoke her father. Grace appeared to be the only one of the party to be listening, as both

Winifred and Harriet were looking over the railing and down to the water below.

Her father turned away from the railing and collided with a crewman.

"Many pardons," spoke the crewmember. He brushed Mr. Hathaway's lapel, and continued to grovel in apologies. Grace noticed that he seemed different from the other officers on deck. He wore a black ship's officer tunic and cap, but it appeared too big for him. Like it belonged to a full-grown man. He appeared clean-shaven, but seemed young—perhaps sixteen or seventeen, and incapable of growing whiskers. The only distinction that made him appear as a man was his height. He was an inch or two above her father's six feet. "Can I be of assistance?" he asked Mr. Hathaway.

"Actually, we are about to see to our rooms up above."

"Right. I'll see you there, myself," he spoke in an English accent, but one that was not as particular and careful as Harriet's.

"That really won't be necessary. I have—"

"It's really no bother," spoke the eager crewman. "Paden Thomas is the name. At your service. 'Ave your ticket, do you?"

Mr. Hathaway pulled his papers from his pocket and flashed them to the young gentleman. Grace assumed that her father was about to inform the fellow that he and Harriet had already travelled the ship on a previous voyage from England. The message would not be given time to be explained.

"Follow me," he said as he straightened his hat on his head of short blonde hair, tilted his head and moved his feet toward the same doorway from which Grace had just come. Grace's father followed directly behind the quick-footed crewman, followed by Harriet, holding her hat on her head and complaining to Winifred about having to move so swiftly in a dress.

Grace followed the others as they ascended the grand staircase once again. She climbed the stairs to the next level and noticed a sign reading, "Upper Promenade Deck". Her head spun in another direction to a brass sign reading, "First Class Passengers Only".

"Right this way, Mr. ...what was it again?"

"Hathaway," returned Grace's father to the young steward.

The party travelled a short distance down a hallway to the right of the staircase where a series of four doors appeared on the left.

Another steward, dressed in the sharp double-breasted tunic, passed the group in the hallway. "Everything all right?" he asked Grace's father, with a smile. He was as tall as Paden, but much stockier, like he were an athlete, and gave each member of the party a square look, giving an air of confidence.

"Just taking these folks to their rooms," Paden responded.

"Well," he said tipping his hat to Harriet, Winifred, and Grace, "let me know if anything shall arise. Steele's the name."

Grace was flattered with his display of charm, but subdued any response when she heard Harriet's fluttering giggle.

"Many thanks, Mr. Steele," she embellished.

Grace and the rest stood aside to allow Mr. Steele to sail down the hall. Grace wasn't certain, but she thought she detected a look from Mr. Steele to Paden. Almost one of disgust, or belittling. She wasn't sure which. His broad shoulders rounded the end of the hall, as the back of his dark head seemed to be shaking at Paden.

"Here you are, Mr. Hathaway," spoke Paden outside the third door. "Now, I see you have this room booked for a Ms. Price and Ms. Duffy."

"My fiancé, Ms. Price, and her Winifred, belong here."

"Very good, sir," spoke Paden as he quickly opened the room door. Grace peeked around his slim stature to see a room with two dark wooden bunks, and a sofa bed. The room appeared small, but was elegant enough. Inside the room were several bags of luggage that she had seen earlier, when Harriet had paid a man at the Toronto train station to cart them around.

"My daughter and I?"

"Your room is straight through the First Class Music Room, right in 'ere, through this doorway."

"My dear, I shall take Grace and show her to our room and give you a chance to settle in," he said to Harriet.

"Very well. We shall come and find you shortly," responded Harriet.

Grace wondered if this whole voyage would be a series of episodes with Harriet keeping her hooks on her father, never allowing him out of her stride.

The sound of a throat clearing was heard. A contrived one. It was Paden.

"Yes, well…" spoke Grace's father. "Lead on."

The young steward led Grace and her father through a wooden door with paned glass and a curtain on the upper half. Grace glanced around the room. There were several tables, some round, some square. Chairs with padded cushions and sofas with rich upholstery and padded footstools. Most notably, sat the Steinway grand piano positioned by a large pillar, just shy of the floor space encompassing the considerably large, domed ceiling of the ship's central shaft. In the background was a lavish fireplace.

"Perhaps, Grace, you could favour us with a selection on the piano later this evening, if the crew shall permit us," spoke her father with a smile, as though he were trying to win her approval.

"A child in the Music Room? It wouldn't be proper," abruptly cranked Harriet's voice as she stabbed her head through the partially open door leading back to her room.

Her father conjured up a smile. "Well, we shall worry about that later," he spoke with his usual lack of defence of Grace.

Paden broke the awkwardness of the moment when he stumbled over a chair that was positioned a little too generously over the rectangular carpet leading to the parallel doorway out of the Music Room. He appeared to drop a dark object, but quickly scampered to the floor to retrieve it before Grace or her father could see what it was. His reddened cheeks exposed his embarrassment.

"Right this way," he spoke with a forced smile, as though nothing had happened.

They moved through another paned door, identical to the one through which they had just passed moments earlier, and found another hallway with doors. Paden made a quick left into a small hall alcove, and then stopped at the only door on his right. He opened the door to reveal a room similar to Harriet's and Winifred's, only this room had a sofa on the left, as well as two beds, one atop the other. Gathered curtains finished each bed. Inside, their luggage was found—laid in precise rows in front of white, double washbasins. Most of their belongings were stored below deck with the "unwanted baggage", which they wouldn't need until their arrival in England.

Grace felt that the room was aesthetically pleasing, with its show of solid wood furnishings and porcelain twin washbasins. However, she couldn't help but think the room was tiny. It could be a long week staying in here with her father.

They entered the room and Grace immediately went to the window to open the curtains so that she could see land. Her land. She wasn't from Quebec City, but it was much closer to home than England, and it would suffice for now.

"Grace, I hope that we…" started her father when he heard another throat clearing. Both he and Grace turned around to see Paden Thomas standing in the doorway, simply smiling. Grace's mind had been so pre-occupied with other things that she had forgotten he was there and apparently, so had her father.

"I'll leave you two be, then," he spoke, staring at the floor in the same awkward manner that he displayed tripping over the chair. Grace almost smiled for the first time since leaving Toronto. There was something about him that she admired. Perhaps, it was his overconfidence, like he was in over his head.

"One moment, sir," spoke her father as he laid his hat on the dresser and reached into his right jacket pocket. "Allow me to…" He appeared to be reaching for his wallet to tip the lad when his head shot up in alarm.

"Is there a problem, sir?" asked Paden.

"My wallet! It is missing! Where could it have gone?"

"You sure, sir?"

"Yes. I had it earlier, right before coming on board. I must have dropped it somewhere. I must look for it immediately."

"I'm sure it'll surface, sir. You'll see. Perhaps, I'll check with the other crew on this deck. See if they've found anything."

"Thank you," spoke Grace's father, patting down the front sides of his jacket with his hands.

"Maybe she…" Grace spoke quietly. "Maybe Harriet somehow has gotten a hold of it."

"That would be odd," returned her father. "In any event, we shall be in dire circumstances if we don't find it. I knew I should have kept some money in the safe with the mine's silver. Nothing would happen to it then." He turned and noticed Paden still in the doorway.

"I shall be on my way," Paden said, straightening his back and raising his chin, as though realizing he was intruding. "Sir. Miss," he spoke, giving each a nod, then exiting.

"Grace, I must go attempt to rescue our money. I will check with Harriet first, then the crew. Will you be all right?"

It was a loaded question. *Was he asking about the next few minutes, or the rest of my life?* she wondered. "Father, I…" she spoke in hesitation. He looked at her, and she in return, looked at him. He stood flustered, once again patted down his front pockets and removed his gaze from her. Her gaze competed with the floor, the jacket, the baggage. He seemed a poor creature—like a lost child.

"I'll be fine, Father. I think I'll go out on deck and get some air."

He nodded, turned around swiftly, and stormed out of the room, probably to cross the Music Room to Harriet and Winifred's room.

Moments later, Grace left her room to return to the deck. Rather than go through the Music Room, the way she came, and risk a meeting with Harriet, she continued down the hallway adjacent to her room. She found a door on the left and went outside. She felt as though she should have taken a sweater, as the late May air seemed to be cooling towards the end of the day. Soon it would be 4:00 and the ship would be leaving. It appeared that she might stand on the deck alone, as the ship left Canada, and as her father was busy saving his money.

Grace stepped across the floor, passing several passengers, male and female, already settled in comfortably on some dark wooden deck chairs. With feet outstretched on the long bodies of the chairs, arms placed on the firm arm rests, several people read, or simply stared at the last portion of land that they would see for about a week. Others sat in the background of the dark alcoves with blankets over their legs, binoculars in hand, or pipes freely dangling from their mouths.

Grace moved down the deck to find a position near the railing towards the aft of the ship, away from the gathering crowd. Her gloves, once again, glided along the smooth railing. She found some isolation and fixed both hands on the railing. Standing on the Upper Promenade Deck, exactly one deck above where she stood moments ago at another similar railing, she looked out, in many directions, at land.

Normally, Grace would be content that the sun was shining. But, now in her spirits, there was dull, grey fog that no sunbeam could penetrate. The empowering river breeze filled her lungs, making her feel as though she were breathing a different air now. Her journey had begun. The Empress of Ireland would steal her away.

She looked down at the gap of water directly below her position, between the pier and the ship. It was a long way down, but Grace could see it clearly enough. The idling of the ship's engines seemed to be moving the water in different directions, creating white foam. It didn't flow in any pattern or cycle or circle. It had no measurable or predictable outcome.

Staring at the water made her think of Andrew. Grace had been in the water that day her cousin died. She could have stopped him from going in, but didn't. When his body was recovered, she was told that the bottom was forty feet down. No way to reach him. But she couldn't forgive herself. She killed her cousin. Her best friend. She knew it. Perhaps, her family knew it.

She wondered now if this water was deep. She leaned over the railing, as though she wanted to get a better look. As she leaned, she considered joining her cousin in the deep. She hadn't been brave enough to go in any water since that day, but something possessed her to ponder it now. She didn't have much to live for. She wouldn't be missed. *Father will move on, like he did with Mother,* she thought. She knew she didn't have the courage to do it. She climbed the metal portion of the railing with her boots, which allowed her to lean over so that the railing tightened against her belly. *Perhaps gravity will make the decision for me,* she thought recklessly.

Grace seemed oblivious to the crowd further up the deck. She didn't matter to them. She didn't matter to anyone. Grace tipped aimlessly over the side.

The Empress of Ireland: Starboard View

Chapter 2

"Oh!" Grace screamed, as she felt a hand against her back pushing her down. A clutch of her dress. A short dip, further over the railing. Back up.

"I've got you. Are you all right?" spoke the young gentleman, removing his hand from Grace's back as she turned around, both feet stumbling to flatten on deck.

"Are you mad?" she yelled, realizing that she was speaking with Paden Thomas, the awkward steward she had just met. "You could have killed me!"

"Seems you were doing a fine job of that yourself, Missy," he retorted in an arrogant tone.

"What are you talking about? I simply slipped a little. I was about to get—"

"Wet, Love. You were about to get wet. I could see 'ow climbin' a railin' could cause you to *slip* like that. 'Sides, is that anyway to treat someone who just saved you?"

"Don't 'Love' me. And I don't need saving," she responded cynically. As she brushed a few straying wisps of her light brown hair which had escaped from her hair bun, away from her eyes, she looked down to make certain that her dress skirt, once again covered her boots.

"Everyone needs savin' at some point in their life. If you don't mind me sayin', Miss, you're not behavin' like a 'well-to-do' young lady, climbin' railins' in a dress, tryin' to kill yourself. You're certainly not as I expected."

"Well, you're not what I expect from a ship's officer. You barely look 15."

"I'm seventeen, Missy. Well, I'll be seventeen come June five."

"Are you sure you're not an impostor, masquerading in uniform?"

"Honourary steward, First Class. Well, Second and Third Class, too, I suppose."

"What does that mean?" inquired Grace with a slight upward curving of her lips. She was starting to become amused, once again, with his demeanour. While he spoke differently, she noticed that his smile seemed to remind her of her cousin Andrew—full of teeth and mischievousness.

"Father is the assistant to the ship's chief steward. He was appointed by Cap'n Kendall himself, only weeks ago. And me? Well, let's just say that I get full run of the ship. They have me fillin' in wherever needs be. I'm quite important around 'ere. I know most of the crew."

That last statement caused Grace to recollect the passing by of Mr. Steele, the steward in the hallway near Harriet and Winifred's room. He somehow seemed dissatisfied with Paden. She raised one eyebrow in disbelief at Paden's story of his command of the ship.

He continued. "Even Cap'n Kendall…I've dined with him on occasion."

"The Captain? And how did you come to be in such a prominent way with the ship and its captain?" Grace noticed that she was being quite assertive, more than usual. She knew she lacked this quality with her father. Perhaps, she was using Paden as a vessel to air her frustration with her current life.

"Well, Missy—"

"Stop calling me that. My name is Grace, if you must."

"I must. Anyway, I 'ave the Crippen Curse to thank for my position on the ship."

"The what?"

"The Crippen...you mean you 'aven't heard of the curse?" Paden began walking up the deck, away from the aft section of the ship, while Grace followed his lead.

"Hawley Harvey Crippen, or 'Doctor' Crippen as he referred to himself, even though he had no real certification as a doctor. He was a weasel of a man who married Cora Turner, or Belle Elmore, the name she went by in London. You see. She was somewhat of a stage actress."

"Somewhat?" questioned Grace.

"Well, you could say, she wasn't so successful. She was given to a promiscuous life of alcohol, and other interests."

"You mean, interests outside of her husband?" asked Grace, blushingly.

"Exactly. And Crippen. He was no St. Peter either. Both spouses lived double lives—one as a marriage partner, and another as a self-seeking commodity. Crippen dressed Cora up in all the finest jewellery, just to give the illusion that he was a successful businessman, not because he loved her or anything."

"So what does this have to do with the Empress of Ireland?" asked Grace.

"I'm gettin' to that. Crippen finally had enough of her, and one day decided to kill Belle, although killin' is a kind word. He slipped her a poison drink, they say, and went on to dispose of her body in pieces, buryin' her in various places.

"Mr. Thomas! That will be all!" she shouted, noticing that passing individuals were taking notice of her and Paden.

"Well, anyway, you could say that Belle was no longer the

whole person he married. Crippen made a convincing case to the Scotland Yard that he had nothing to do with her disappearance and managed to avoid them for a while. That is, until they found evidence in the cellar.

"Evidence?" asked Grace with a tone of scepticism.

"You don't want to know," continued Paden. "Well, anyway, enter Cap'n Kendall into the story. Turns out, Crippen made a voyage on board a Canadian Pacific ship called the Montrose, Cap'n Kendall's former ship. One of the crew alerted Cap'n Kendall about a mysterious man travelling with his teenage son. The crewman noticed the son had a small stature, being that he looked somewhat like a young lady. The Cap'n investigated and discovered that the mysterious passengers were in fact, Crippen and his latest lady friend."

"What did the Captain do?"

"A series of wireless messages were sent back and forth to Scotland Yard. As news of the imminent arrest reached the public newspapers, several wireless messages were sent to the Montrose for Crippen himself, warning him of his soon arrest. The Cap'n had to keep Crippen busy, and even entertain him personally so that he would be distracted enough and not receive the wireless warnings. Crippen was arrested at Father Point, where incidentally, we will be stopping later tonight, to drop off our pilot. He was arrested and finally, a curse was placed on Cap'n. Crippen fell to the deck in front of Cap'n Kendall and vowed, 'You will suffer for this treachery, sir.'"

"That's quite the interesting story, Paden, but how do you come to be aboard the Empress because of it?" Grace asked, still with a puzzled expression.

"The Cap'n became quite the hero as a result of an important tip from a clever crewman."

"Let me guess," interjected Grace. "The clever crewman was—"

"My father. Cap'n Kendall became our cap'n aboard the Empress only weeks ago. This is his maiden voyage. As soon as he learned that Father was on the crew manifest, he immediately promoted him from the lower decks to Cap'n's Assistant Chief Steward. And me, well, let's just say I have advanced too."

"So, let me see if I have this straight. Crippen was pretending to be a doctor, and married a woman, all the while they both behaved as though they were not married. Then Crippen and his lady both disguised themselves to avoid capture from the Captain who actually pretended to entertain the good doctor. And now, you are in disguise, pretending to be some sort of 'free-to-roam-the-ship steward', having been assimilated by the crew.

"It's no disguise, Grace. Really. I'm a well-respected part of this crew. You'll see."

"Really? That's not what I sensed from that crewman in the hallway, near our rooms. You didn't seem to impress him."

"Who? Steele? You pay no never-mind to him. He's full of 'imself. He's after my father's job. Tha's all. He thought he was up for promotion, that is, until father came along. He's just bitter."

"I see," spoke Grace, softening her tone, as she felt she was sounding too judgmental. Grace noticed for the first time since moving to the aft part of the Upper Promenade Deck, that she had followed Paden further up the deck, back towards the other passengers. Each man and woman seemed as though they were dressed for a tea party or a formal evening dinner. Ladies carrying parasols, and men with cigars or pipes, all 'dressed to the nines', ushering their female companions along.

"Our First Class isn't as busy this time 'round. It'll be a lighter run for the crew up 'ere," spoke Paden as he gazed around at the passers-by. "And speaking of disguise, there's Laurence Irving."

"Who?" Grace innocently asked. She looked to see a man and a woman, probably in their forties, strolling together. The man had a slim moustache, dark hair, and wore a black opera-style cape over a fur-collared overcoat, highlighted by a silk scarf.

"I'm surprised you 'aven't heard of him. I hadn't myself, not being a man of cultured theatre-going, like you probably are...except that you're a woman, and indeed not a man," stumbled Paden.

Grace almost challenged Paden on his being a grown 'man', but chose to let him continue.

"According to several crew mates, he's extremely famous in England. Canada, too. He just finished a Canadian tour. I imagine he doesn't want people crowdin' him aboard ship."

"He has a strange manner of disguise if he doesn't wish to be noticed," Grace said, in reference to his flamboyant attire. She paused. "It's all a disguise, isn't it?" she muttered under her breath.

"Excuse me?" questioned Paden.

"They're all wearing disguises aren't they? They're all clouded in masks of vanity. Pretending that First Class makes them better citizens. That wealth holds all the answers." Grace thought of her father's pursuit of fortune through his impending marriage to Harriet when she spoke these words. She looked around at the wealthy passengers beginning to escape out on deck.

"Dim moon-eyed fishes near
Gaze at the gilded gear, and query:
'What does this vaingloriousness down here?'"

"What was that?" spoke the puzzled young man. "I didn't catch any of that at all. Didn't get that far in school, you know."

"Sorry," responded Grace. "It's part of a poem by Thomas Hardy. I studied it in school. It's about the Titanic." Grace waved her hand at Paden, as if to say, 'never mind'. "How can you stand it? Catering to their every whim?" she asked, gesturing with her head at the passengers around them.

"It's all about giving them what they want, isn't it?" he answered.

"Isn't that costly in itself? Costly to you?" she pressed. She couldn't help but think of what her passiveness with her father was costing her.

Paden turned towards the railing and looked out over the buildings in the distance. Grace turned with him. "Before I left to come aboard the Empress, Mother told me a story about an architect by the name of Christopher Wren. It seems he designed the Windsor Town Hall, near London, a couple hundred years ago. He built a ceilin' that was supported by large pillars. When the town officials came to inspect the place, they weren't happy. They believed the building to be unsafe—that the ceilin' would come down. And so, they ordered the man to put in more pillars."

Grace wished to ask Paden about his mother's whereabouts now, and why he wasn't with her, but felt he should finish the story. "What did he do?"

Paden turned to Grace with a smile. "He gave them what they wanted. He built another four pillars. Only these ones didn't quite reach the ceilin'. They only gave the appearance of support. In fact, Mother says they still stand today and act as a bit of a tourist sight." Looking at Grace directly with his brown eyes, Paden continued. "So you see, my dear Grace, that's become my role here. And Father's also. Caterin' to the whims of those who don't know any better than we."

Grace was beginning to feel sorry for this boy whom she had only met within the last hour, but with whom she had much in common. They were both playing a game of trying to please.

Grace heard a laugh. She turned to see Laurence Irving jesting with another First Class patron who was holding a wine glass.

Paden interrupted Grace's gaze across the deck. "What about you, Grace?"

"What about me?" she answered.

"What is your disguise? Who are you tryin' to please?"

As much as Grace would have liked a confidant, she was not eager to divulge information to someone she had only recently made an acquaintance. She would have liked to tell him about her mother, and the happy life she and her family used to lead. About her father, stealing her away to a foreign land. A small part of her imagined that telling him might give her an ally. Someone who would say, "You're right. That is awful. You should do something about that." He had obviously left his homeland to travel abroad. He wouldn't understand her longing to remain near her mother. Her aunt. Her Canada.

"That's funny," spoke Paden.

"What is?" asked Grace.

"Look," said Paden pointing to land.

Grace followed the guidance of Paden's hand towards what appeared to be a storage shed by the docks. It had '27' posted on the side. She looked to its roof and noticed an orange tabby cat.

"That's Emmy. Our cat. She's been with the ship for the past two years."

"Looks like she has immigrated to Canada now," said Grace.

"I s'pose so. Strange. Wonder why she jumped ship."

"Maybe she—"

"Shh. Listen," said Paden, interrupting Grace by placing his index finger to his mouth.

"What is it?" Grace asked. She strained to hear over the faint rumbling of the ship, and the chatter of passengers around her. *It sounds like...it sounds like, 'O Canada',* she thought.

"I believe it's the Sally Army," spoke Paden.

"The what?"

"The Salvation Army. Come with me." He tugged her arm while her heels made a fast clicking as they moved up the deck. "Down 'ere. Be careful going down."

He led her down a set of steps, about halfway up the deck. They emerged on the Lower Promenade Deck and glided past stateroom windows towards the bow of the ship. Some passengers moved with them towards the activity at the front. Others stood still, showing no response at all. As they made their way further to the bow, definite sounds of the recognizable tune were heard and increased in brightness and brilliance.

"There," he pointed.

As Grace looked down past the approaching stairway to the bow, she saw a group of brightly uniformed men, seated in a semi-circle, wearing Stetsons and holding shiny instruments. The last line of the patriotic tune had been played as passengers, already situated below, and those up on the ascending two decks, leaning over railings, broke out in applause. Grace looked down to notice crowds of well-wishers on the docks, echoing the applause and waving to many on the ship. Some of them flew hand-held Union Jacks.

Grace looked back at the red tunics. She had seen them from a distance at the train station in Toronto. She didn't know who they were really. They looked like the Royal North West Mounted Police. She saw them board the train, but that was the last she thought of them. The little she knew about The Salvation Army was from her mother. She knew they were a church group who reached out to people in need. That was about it. As she listened to the playing of 'Auld Lang Syne', she marvelled at the tuneful playing, being a musician herself. Their leader, a man who appeared in his thirties, smiled at the crowd through his moustache, as he waved his arm in a flowing fashion through every beat of the familiar strain.

"I bet you didn't count on a free concert, eh Grace?" smiled Paden.

Grace stepped down the final steps and followed Paden towards the band. They were about eight feet away. She had seen a band perform in a Toronto park once, when she visited her Aunt Nona. However, she hadn't been this close to a music group of this quality before. Grace immediately felt a connection with the group. Perhaps it was the notion of having a part of her country travel with her for the next week. It would make her feel like part of her home was still present. "They're wonderful," she said.

"They're all right, I s'pose. Groups like this are on every street corner in London. It's almost 4:25," spoke Paden above a melody that Grace recognized, but couldn't think of the name. "It seems we are running a little late. I think the late arrival of the train threw us off. Not to mention the Sally Ann, probably slowin' us up with all their baggage and instruments."

Grace noticed that Paden almost seemed disgusted through his raised upper lip, and lowered tone of voice. She continued to look around and noticed that there were other Salvationists, as she had once heard her mother call them, standing around, watching the band and mingling with the ship folk. The men were dressed in high collar black tunics that appeared to choke them, although their faces gave no hint of this. There was an "S" badge on either side of their neck at the front. Their heads were topped with caps that looked similar to those worn by some of the ship's officers, only they were black, and had a red band encircling them, reading "The Salvation Army", and a maple leaf badge, top and centre. There were ladies present, also. They too, wore dark outfits, but with long dresses. Some of them had the maple leaf emblazoned on the centre of their necks, and some wore bonnets.

"Are your sins washed?" spoke a clear voice. Grace turned her head to see if the words were meant for her.

"What?" asked Paden in an agitated tone.

"Are you saved?" continued the man. He was silver-haired, presented a dusty white moustache and beard, and wore round spectacles and a hearty smile.

"What's that supposed to mean?" asked Paden, standing back a small step and using the same bothered tone of voice.

"I think he means your soul. Are your sins forgiven?" spoke Grace. Grace had been to church regularly growing up, until her mother died. She was familiar with some of the hymns and figurative language.

Paden grew even more agitated. "I don't need savin', man," he returned. "I'm fine, just as I am!"

"We all need to know the grace of God, my young man," spoke the man gently.

"Look," returned Paden, not backing down, "the only Grace I have ever known is standing in front of me.

Grace was slightly embarrassed. She was surprised at the bluntness of the older man, but didn't want him to think that she was a heathen, or that she shared the same offence as Paden. She had only met Paden a short while ago, and still didn't really know him.

"Didn't you tell me, only moments ago, that 'everyone needs savin' at some point in their life'?" she said to Paden, mimicking his accent and tone.

"I'm sorry," apologized the Salvationist. "I didn't mean to intrude, but I would ask that you consider your eternity."

Paden took a large breath and was about to respond with full intent, until Grace spoke again to intercept any harsh remarks. "What is that melody that the band is playing now?" she asked. The band had only played a few bars of music when Grace noticed the land was moving. There was a slight rumbling beneath her feet, and she realized the ship had cast off.

"It's called, 'God Be With You, Till We Meet Again'," spoke the older gentleman. Grace nodded in response and simply listened, while Paden began peering around in a restless fashion. Many people lined the railings waving down to those on the docks. Grace couldn't help but hear the man singing softly.

"God be with you till we meet again
Keep love's banner floating o'er you
Strike death's threatening wave before you
God be with you till we meet again."

"What a lovely thought that is," spoke Paden sarcastically, in response to the words of the hymn. "These people are barmy," spoke Paden to Grace, with a quick shake of his head and a scowl on his face. "I'm off," he said, and turned to leave, but bumped into the man with the beard. It reminded her of the moment when Paden bumped into her father, only this time, he did not apologize. There was a brief shuffle of bodies, then Paden broke free, allowing Grace only to see the back of his head marching back up the stairs.

That was abrupt, thought Grace. She realized that she was once again, alone. Except for the stranger who had set Paden off. He was that. A stranger. Her father wanted to be with her for the "grand send-off". Now it was Grace. All on her own. *So, this is how it will be*, she thought.

She watched the land moving slowly towards the stern of the ship. Dodging stationary people, she walked back towards the stairs. Instant thoughts came to her. *One last chance. Where's the gangway? I must get off.* She moved faster, gradually making her way down the Lower Promenade Deck. She realized the land was slowing down as she kept up with it, moving the opposite direction of the ship. She imagined if she ran, that she would get ahead, and her comfort of home would last longer. *But, that would be silly. Only temporary. Stupid*, she chided herself for her momentary panic. It was already too late, the moment she stepped aboard. She would never see home again.

Grace slowed down to a walk. She stopped looking on land and focused her gaze on the deck floor. She shuffled aimlessly by small pockets of people perched near the railing. She continued until she reached the last section of the Lower Promenade Deck that was covered overhead. She now overlooked the stern of the ship. There she noticed a large mast, towering the sky with a light atop. The mast carried a cable high across the ship to the bow, where Grace noticed the tip of a twin mast at the bow. The masts extended far above the twin funnels in the top centre of the ship. *What an enormous ship,* Grace thought.

About to turn around and return to her room on the Upper Promenade Deck, Grace heard a raised voice above the breeze. "Stop making excuses!" said the angry voice. Grace focused her attention towards the stern. Then towards a lifeboat to the left.

"I'm not making excuses!" returned another voice.

Grace looked at the back of the lifeboat and saw a head popping over the canvas cover. It was Paden's. Grace ducked behind the metal base of the mast. She looked behind her to see only a few passengers nearby. Most were along the sides and towards the bow, and oblivious of her. She looked back and saw the angry voice was coming from a slightly heavyset man. He did not wear a ship's uniform, appeared dirty with some sort of black soot on his face, and had Paden in his clutches at the chest. He was shaking Paden and yelled something that Grace couldn't make out. The ship's horn blasted, catching Grace off-guard and causing her to let out a scream. She covered her mouth and ducked down behind the structure, looking up towards the aft funnel, where the sudden noise appeared to be originating. Then, slowly standing, after composing herself, she looked to see that the two men had disappeared.

Canada's Salvation Army Staff Band,
picture taken just prior to trip aboard the Empress

Chapter 3

Grace's dress swirled at the bottom as she spun in search of the two missing figures. *Did they know I was listening? Will they appear out of nowhere and see me lurking behind the base of the mast,* she wondered. She saw only passengers making their way along the starboard deck, and a few looking out from the stern. She felt it best to leave and return to her room. *Perhaps Father will be there,* she thought.

Making her way up the starboard side, she entered a set of double doors closer to the bow of the ship. Immediately, she found the grand staircase and ascended one flight to her deck. As she entered the hallway where Harriet and Winifred were accommodated, Grace had a sick feeling that she might encounter Harriet. She knew she couldn't avoid her for the entire journey, but needed some space for the time being.

No Harriet. Vacant corridor. Clear sailing through the Music Room and back to her and her father's room. She knocked lightly, but heard no response. She entered the empty room and sat on the sofa. There was nothing to do but wait. Wait and wonder. *Where could Father be? Has he noticed that he has misplaced me, as well as his wallet?*

Grace decided to reach into the front section of her baggage still sitting in the middle of the room, and pull out a book she had started to read on the train: "The Mystery of Wilkshire Mansion". She had brought it along to attempt a distraction from her current predicament. Grace enjoyed mysteries. She marvelled at how difficult it could be for the reader to solve the crime, even though clues were placed in the way. Only after reading, would she realize the clues had been there all along. And Grace discovered a somewhat reliable way of determining the identity of the villain before the end. The villain always turned out to be the least-likely person you would suspect. Choose that person. No matter how inconceivable it appeared, chances are, that is the one on whom you should focus.

Grace pulled out her train ticket that doubled as a bookmark and started mid-way through the chapter where she left off. About halfway through the novel, she tried to recall the main characters to be considered. *Winston, the gardener. He seemed implausible. He had nothing to gain. Perhaps he was the one. Aunt Ruth. She couldn't have done it. She was out of town. So, maybe she did it, after all.*

Grace quickly realized that she was thinking in contradictions. She pulled her mind out of her book as swiftly as she had plunged into it. Events of the afternoon troubled her: her father leaving her for his wallet; Paden leaving her for a meeting with a stranger. Something seemed amiss. It was like another mystery unravelling. *Only, the fictional kind in books are more exciting, and less annoying,* she thought. Still, the events of the day did set the tone for what could be an interesting week at sea.

Focus on the implausible, she thought again. Grace's attempts to focus on the book were interrupted by thoughts of her father and Paden. Her father said that he had his wallet with him just before coming aboard. When Grace came aboard with the others, one of the first people she met was Paden. *In fact, Paden literally bumped into Father,* she remembered. Turning her eyes away from the book,

Grace looked at the door of her room and envisioned the Music Room. Paden had escorted her and her father across the room. He made a clumsy dive to pick up something he had dropped. *Could Paden have stolen Father's wallet?* It was a silly thought. *It is too convenient a solution. It is too unrealistic. It is too…implausible.*

Grace wanted to ponder the thought some more, but was distracted by voices outside her room. It was her father and Harriet. Harriet employed her usual agitated voice. Grace stood and crept towards the door to hear a little better.

"Jeremiah, it wouldn't be appropriate."

"But it has to be."

"She's just a child. People in First Class don't want a child to dine with them. And besides, you have been invited to dine at the Captain's table. That is a rare honour."

"What shall become of her, then?"

"She shall eat in the Children's Saloon, where she belongs."

Grace was starting to get accustomed to Harriet's devising ways of getting rid of her. Still, she hoped that her father would not bend.

"Perhaps, I shall speak to a steward, quickly before dinner. See what arrangements can be made that will be…mutually acceptable, dear."

Grace's father had a wise business sense. He was always making plans. Always on the move. A quick engagement. A quick voyage. "Up the ramp, quickly, Grace. I must quickly find my wallet. Talk to the steward quickly." So far, he had deferred Harriet's pleas against Grace. *How long would Harriet stand it?* wondered Grace. Grace was starting to envision being seated at a tiny table with giggly infants needing their noses wiped. She adored children, but didn't want to be seen as a helpless child herself.

The conversation seemed to lull, and Grace stepped away from the door with the expectation of its opening.

"Grace, my dear. You're here?" exclaimed her father with full white eyes as he opened the door.

"Where have you been, child?" stammered Harriet, as she squeezed her way into the partially opened door. "We were looking for you about the ship."

Grace responded in a soft tone. "But, I thought you were looking for—"

"We shan't be kept occupied all week wondering where you are," chided the woman. Grace thought that if her father had spoken, he would have said 'worrying where you are.' Harriet was more concerned with her own affairs.

"The dinner hour is still some time away. Time for you to go freshen up and change, my dear?" interrupted her father to Harriet. While he had difficulty in making a stand for Grace, he was perfecting the deferring tactic—pushing the lid down on things to keep them kept. Grace believed that Harriet would only tolerate this behaviour for so long. She would force him to make firm decisions about his daughter. She would take him into uncharted waters.

"Regardless, I believe Grace looks exhausted. Why don't you rest for a little while?" suggested her father.

Grace nodded in agreement. She had not quite recovered from last night's train ride from Toronto, having left after midnight and travelled all through the night.

Waking up while slouched on the sofa in her room, Grace hadn't realized she had fallen asleep. Her father had gone, as well as Harriet, and she soaked up the silence. Perhaps the gentle vibrating movement of the ship had rocked her into a slumber.

She looked at her watch. 7:05. *I should arise, or I will miss dinner*, she thought to herself in a waking daze. Sitting up, not quite ready to stand, Grace peered out through the window above the padded sofa. She had to part the curtain slightly. Her view of green fields, rolling landscape, and frequent rooftops, was interrupted slightly by the walking by of passenger bodies at her window and a dimming skyline. Land was still in sight. Her land. At least for a little while longer until it became darker and before the ship emerged out of the St. Lawrence River, deep into the Atlantic.

She stood and straightened out her dress and felt her hair for signs of compromise to its neatness. She bundled up her hair into a bun and secured it with a few pins from her toiletry bag that lay beside one of the washbasins. She checked her compact mirror to ensure that she fit the part of a First Class lady, and not a giddy schoolgirl. *Most of the other passengers in First Class will probably have changed their clothes for dinner*, she thought, but felt she was in good standing as is.

Grace left the room, not knowing exactly where she would be dining. The First Class Dining Saloon? The Children's Saloon? She hadn't the opportunity to find either, nor hear whether her father had resolved the issue with Harriet. Carrying her novel with her, just in case she was to be dining alone, Grace decided to start walking and see if she ran into her father. She stepped into the hallway and strutted to the main staircase. She decided to go down. As she approached the stairs, she recalled seeing what she thought was the dining room, upon first arriving on the ship and starting up the stairs.

"Are you lost?" asked a handsome, dark-haired steward in a black tunic with epaulets, who appeared on the staircase from below. Looking down on him from above, she recognized him immediately as Mr. Steele, the friendly steward from earlier in the hallway—but not friendly towards Paden, for some reason.

"D...Dining Saloon," stuttered Grace, sounding a little nervous. She realized that she wasn't sure which saloon she was meant to go to, and whether she should like Mr. Steele, based on Paden's earlier comments.

"Why don't I take you there myself, Miss?" he said with a raised elbow, gesturing for her to envelop her arm inside his. Grace smiled, and heard a small giggle come out. *I hope he didn't hear that*, she thought in alarm. She was starting to act like Harriet upon meeting Mr. Steele for the first time. He had a natural charm, to be certain.

Mr. Steele led Grace down the remaining few stairs to the Lower Promenade Deck, and then continued down to the next level. She recognized this deck as the Shelter Deck where she had come aboard. She was beginning to acquaint herself with the ship's layout and felt a little more confident with locations. They stepped off the last stair and walked a short left to a set of double doors. Grace could see through the approaching panes that there were long rectangular tables inside, and many finely dressed guests standing or sitting nearby.

In advance of the door, Grace saw a tunic open the door from the inside to allow her and Mr. Steele to enter. She stole a quick look and almost looked away from the crewman, but realized she knew him. It was Paden. Only, it was a different Paden. He looked official in his stance at the door and gave no hint of his abrupt disappearance and subsequent scuffle with the mystery man.

"'Ello," he said to Grace with a smile, pointing his toes together and nodding his head towards the floor. The smile immediately disappeared as he made eye contact with Officer Steele. "Mr. Steele," he spoke with a hint of a nod, but no suggestion of a grin.

"I believe I found something of yours, Mr. Thomas," spoke Mr. Steele, signalling a tilted head nod towards Grace, but not losing Paden's eyes. "I'm quite certain you were to be positioned upstairs on the upper decks, assisting passengers with their dinner table assignments. Is that not right, Mr. Thomas?"

The firm stare alone would have intimidated the lad, let alone the words, thought Grace.

"Well, sir," responded Paden, with no apparent wound to his image, "we shall not keep the lady waiting further, shall we?"

Mr. Steele shook his head, tightened his lips, then turned and walked back out the doors.

Paden motioned his head further into the First Class Dining Saloon for Grace to follow. He did not invite her to take his arm, as Officer Steele had. It seemed he lacked some of the higher qualities of experienced crewmen. At first, neither said anything. Paden gazed around at the various tables as though he did not know what to do, and Grace simply took in all her surroundings.

She stepped forward a number of steps in order to pass by a wall on her right. It appeared to be part of a square-shaped structure, and she figured it must house one of the ship's large funnels. Rounding the corner of the wall, she noticed an upright piano at the start of a carpeted aisle that ran the length of the room. How she would love to make contact with its ivory keys, later on. Her gaze was attracted to the bright white enamel ceilings and the various sculptured moldings. The ship's central well opened up a ceiling that revealed hints of the First Class Café above. Seeing people line the railings gave Grace a sense that she was being observed from above, like an audience studying players in the theatre. The entire room was predominantly adorned in rich mahogany, from the doors, chairs, and alcove seating areas to the sides. Each table in the room had meticulously placed table settings, from cutlery to napkins to fine china dishes. *Someone must have spent much of the afternoon laying these out,* she thought.

The outer edges of the room consisted of semi-circular tables inset in alcoves. The alcoves each had two large portholes that were augmented with stained glass windows. Grace also noticed some serving tables that were manned by several crewmen. The room sparkled with the use of electric light globes hanging from the ceiling. The emerging quiet darkness outside the room's walls was silenced by their incandescent glow and the quiet strains of melody being performed by five musicians, holding stringed instruments near the central well.

Grace decided to break the silence between her and Paden first. "Well, you made off rather quickly," she said with a hint of suspicion. "Something important to do?"

"Some ship's business, as usual," he returned, straightening his jacket as though it were a poor fit, and not making eye contact.

"What business is that?" she questioned. "Being abrupt with the passengers?" Grace hoped Paden would realize how rude he had been with the Salvation Army man earlier. "Helping yourself to—" Grace was about to make a serious accusation about her father's wallet. She had suspicions, but realized they could be part of her fragile imagination. Perhaps she had read too many mysteries, like the one she still held in her hand.

"What are you talking about, woman?" responded Paden with another hint of the annoyance she had witnessed earlier on deck with the older gentleman.

Grace felt it best to change subjects. She was beginning to wonder if she belonged in the room. Was she supposed to go the Children's Saloon? Where was her father? She began to ask about her father. "Have you seen—"

"Over 'ere," spoke Paden. He stepped away from Grace and walked towards a table on the right, towards the rear of the room, just shy of the alcoves. As she followed, she noticed her father and Harriet sitting at the table. They had both changed into formal eveningwear. Her father wore a black swallowtail suit, and Harriet presented a blood-red fabric from neck to toe, adorned with a flashy necklace and earrings. The jewellery might have saved the dress enough to distract the viewers of its strong, awful colour.

"Good evening, Grace," spoke her father, who turned and stood as his daughter reached the table. "I hope you rested. I see you made your way down all right."

Grace nodded, and noticed Harriet seated and silent, arms crossed, as though she wanted to speak against Grace being there, but her father continued.

"We have room at the Captain's table here if you like, although it seems the Captain will not be joining us this evening." Grace looked around at some empty chairs, but noticed other finely dressed couples seated, looking up at Grace with polite smiles. Her father mentioned some of the names by way of introduction to Grace and she nodded politely. "Clayton Burt. Mrs. Dunlevy. And of course, our famous Irving couple. Grace, do you know who..." Her father stopped speaking when he realized the Irvings had already risen from the table and were making their way over to the rear alcove off to the right. Grace assumed they had changed tables when they learned the captain would not be joining them.

"End of Act I, I suppose," spoke her father, trying to be witty, in response to the hasty departure of the famous couple.

"If you should need anything, sir, I'll..." spoke Paden.

Her father woke from his distraction and realized Grace was still standing. "Grace, dear. I'm sorry to forget about you. You are welcome to sit with us, or if you like, perhaps Mr. Thomas could keep you company at one of these spare tables."

Grace noticed that the room seemed rather empty in comparison to the number of tables available. She remembered Paden's comment on how the First Class numbers were lacking for this crossing.

Paden spoke. "Oh, I'm 'fraid that's impossible, sir. I have my duties to—"

"Is not looking after the First Class passengers part of your responsibilities, young man?"

Grace was certain she was turning red in the cheeks. She felt a hard swallow in her throat. She didn't wish to sit down with Paden at this time. She didn't trust him. "Father, I think that Mr. Thomas is too busy for—"

"Mr. Thomas, please. I can speak to your superior, if you like. You are the closest person to Grace's age here, and I think it would be helpful to her if you could join her. Wouldn't it, Grace?"

Grace forced a smile and nodded in the affirmative. Her polite compliance was becoming too much of a liturgical habit.

"Splendid, then," spoke her father swiftly. "How can I repay you, good man? Grace, did you know that Mr. Thomas found my wallet?"

Grace sobered her gazed towards her father. "Your wallet?"

"Yes. Here it is," spoke her father as he slipped the wallet from his inner suit pocket. "He found it lying outside on deck. Not a bill missing, either. I must have carelessly dropped it when we arrived. I shall make certain it goes in the safe with the mine's silver, later on."

Grace was confused. She had allowed her imagination to get the best of her. How silly it was of her to get caught up in mysteries, as though they were real. She had behaved like...like a child. She finally spoke to Paden. "Mr. Thomas," she said with a genuine smile, "I would like to join you this evening, if that is all right with you."

Paden's face seemed to warm up to the notion, and he walked to an empty table, two over, next to the set of alcove tables along the starboard windows. Once again, he walked. Grace followed. No gracious lead or escort. Simply, follow Paden, or get left behind. Paden then sat, and gestured with his hand towards a crimson leather chair, rather than pull it out and assist her in her seat. *He has poor qualities for a gentleman,* thought Grace as she wondered how he ever survived his employer. *Perhaps, this is why he has not pleased Mr. Steele.*

Grace sat for a moment listening to the ship's quintet. She thought she recognized the song being played, but couldn't associate a title to the joyous strains. She struggled for words to say to Paden. He seemed to be pre-occupied as he awkwardly glanced around the room. Sensing his lack of interest in conversation, she decided to crack open her book to the page she had been reading, and continued on. *'The most successful of crimes', spoke Mr. Kimberly to the others, 'are those that are committed with partial truths. That way, the culprit may capitalize on the truth, in order to mask the deception.'*

Paden stole Grace from her fantasy world of reading when he finally broke the silence. "What ya' reading?"

"A mystery. About a murder…in a mansion." She raised the cover and flashed it in his direction. "It's by Post. Have you heard of him?"

Shaking his head, he responded. "I'm afraid I'm not much of a reader. 'Less of course, it's a menu, cuz' I'm starved."

Grace was not impressed with his attempt at humour, but then saw no indication of a smile. *Is he serious?*

He continued, straight-faced. "Read much?"

"All the time," came the response. "It helps me keep a balance. Whenever I feel discouraged, reading distracts me."

Paden must have thought that he was the cause of discouragement to Grace, as he softened his eyes. "Listen, Grace. About earlier, on the deck. I want to apologize 'bout my behaviour. It's just that—"

"It's all right, Paden. I understand," responded Grace instantly, without allowing Paden time to offer some sort of explanation. She was too quick to appease. A habit that she had to cast off immediately. The truth was, she didn't understand. She didn't know who the other man was that wished Paden serious harm, and what trouble he might be in. Perhaps, she could help Paden. She certainly didn't want to pry and receive the same response from Paden that she witnessed on deck with the older gentleman. However, it was Paden who set the arising tone of inquiry.

"Grace, if you don't mind my asking, what's with the uptight lady? Miss Priss, I believe. Is she a relative or something?"

"Miss Price." Grace smiled, realizing that Paden had perceptively picked up on Harriet's faulty personality in only two short meetings. "She is…" Grace wondered how much she should divulge. It could be a long week aboard the ship if she couldn't confide with at least one person she felt comfortable with. Her father was right. Paden was close to her age, and she had previously felt that he somehow mirrored her cousin, Andrew. She would choose to open up to him. "She is my mother-to-be. My father is marrying her shortly after we arrive in England."

"What 'appened to your real mother?" he asked matter-of-factly.

"She's dead," spoke Grace directly. "Died about a year ago of tuberculosis."

"I'm sorry to hear that," responded Paden with a hint of sympathetic expression in his voice. "And your new mother…how do you feel about that?"

"Not very well, indeed," she answered. "My father seems more interested in keeping up the social cues, than looking after his daughter. Harriet will look after him for life. Look after his wallet, that is."

"How do you mean?" he asked, seeming somewhat caught off-guard.

"Let's just say he allowed much of our fortune to slip away."

Grace went on to explain about her father's funding of her mother's mission project. She also spoke of extra expenses that were needed to help her mother through her illness—medicines, a nurse, funeral arrangements. As Grace verbalized her past, she wondered if her father had thought that his wife had caused them much misery by all her medical expenses. *Was he that displeased with her?*

"I heard that your father is responsible for a load of silver bars on board," asked Paden.

"You did? How did—"

"Word travels quickly on a ship like this," he answered. "But, your father must be doing well financially if his employer put him in charge of that kind of loot."

Grace thought his choice of the word 'loot' was curious. "Father is hoping to make some influential contacts in England through Harriet's father. When he shows up with all that silver to deliver, no doubt her father will be impressed with the responsibility entrusted in him. As a banker, he will appreciate that and see to it that he is secured with a prominent position."

"And if he were to misplace his silver, like he did his wallet?" asked Paden with a smile.

"Then, we would probably end up back in Cobalt, Ontario, at the mercy of Father's mining company, and seeking help from the very mission Mother had founded."

Grace noticed a waiter deliver some bread to her and Paden's table. He said nothing as he dropped the bread and continued on, giving Paden a second glance. Grace figured he was wondering why Paden was sitting with the passengers, about to enjoy a meal prepared for passengers. Grace didn't think too much of it, and continued the conversation.

"And what of you, Paden? You mentioned your father. Where is your mother?"

"Sure I do. Her name's Elise. Elise Thomas. She lives in the East end of London…well, we all do—that is my parents and me, when we're together."

"Are there problems between your parents?"

"No. Nothing like that. They get along all right. It's just that times have been a li'l rough. Mother works hard cleaning houses for a string of rich folk, and Father and I…well, we have to go at it here at sea."

"Do you get to see her very often?" asked Grace with a look of concern.

"Oh, sure. Nearly every time we go back and forth with the crossing. We spend a day or two together, before the next trip."

"That isn't much of a family life? How do you cope?"

"Family life? There'll be lots of time for that later. Right now, Father and I have to make a bit of money, get settled a bit financially. Father promised Mother that we'd be done this life in a few years and we can settle again in London, together."

"Years?" asked Grace with full blue eyes. Grace had struggled for less than that time being apart from her mother. She couldn't imagine coping with Paden's family situation, particularly when, ultimately, they had a choice. Money might be in wanting, but certainly, they could find another way. They could stay together as a family.

Paden brushed back a small, short clump of his blond hair that slipped forward on his forehead. "No worries," he continued. "I don't think it'll be that long. I think we'll be back together sooner, than later. In the meantime, Father and I will have to continue on, looking after the spoiled lot who pay our way with their frivolity and careless spending."

Grace pulled back her shoulders, tilted her head, and gave Paden a look that he perceptively read immediately.

"Well, present company exempted, of course," he said with a concocted smile.

Grace was becoming famished as she had not eaten since coming aboard. She picked up a dinner roll from a basket on the table. She felt awkward maneuvering anything from its position on the table. Everything set just right. *Some poor fellow earns a wage by strategically laying the glasses. The cutlery. The flowers. And even the neatly folded napkins,* she thought. *Hours of work, only to be dismantled in seconds. What a shame.* About to apply a piece of the swirl-sculpted butter to her roll, she noticed a crewman approaching her table from the rear of the room. He had just come through a set of double wooden doors. She had witnessed his faint silhouette in the door window at first, and now in the room, it seemed he was on a collision course with her and Paden. He was uniformed, appeared in his early forties, had light brown hair, and wore a turned down mouth.

"Paden," he spoke angrily, giving Paden a jolt from his seat. "What manner is this? Shouldn't you be—"

"I was just entertaining a guest, sir. I was trying to—"

"You're not here to entertain," growled the man as he stole a quick glance down at Grace, then back onto Paden who was now standing fully. "If it's entertainment you wish, then entertain the notion of all the lavatories on the ship that need cleaning, and who will be doing it, if you don't get back to duty."

"Aye, sir. Right away, sir," spoke Paden, standing stiff with arms by his sides. He immediately raised his right hand to his brow, but his salute was ignored. The man had stopped only momentarily, and continued on his destructive path by snapping at a couple of other crewman along his way before exiting the room through the front doors by the grand staircase.

Grace was astonished with the man's disposition. Everyone else working on this ship had such a nice demeanor—with the exception of Paden's mysterious enemy down on deck, by the lifeboat. The remainder of the crew was so helpful and friendly.

Grace looked up at Paden whose facial expression showed signs that his wall of inner pride had been carved open with a glancing blow, like a heavy steel blade through tin.

"What a monster!" she blurted out to Paden. "Who is that awful man?"

"That man," he answered, "that man is my father."

The First Class Dining Saloon

Chapter 4

"Your father?" questioned Grace. She had been caught off-guard and was without words.

"Yes, and that is why I must go."

"But—" interjected Grace.

"I'm sorry to leave you again, but I have duties I must attend to," spoke Paden, staring at the carpet, never once looking at Grace. He pushed his chair into the table, and made off, exiting through the same door as his father.

Alone, once again, thought Grace. She felt that fate was leading her on a course of solitude. Abandoned by her father with his wife-to-be and left alone on deck. Abandoned by Paden on deck. Now, abandoned at the dinner table. *It appears that someone's efforts will be in vain this evening,* she thought, surveying the untouched laid-out cutlery and stand-up tepee napkins at her empty table. *I can't stay here, alone,* she thought. She looked around at the sea of people dining. While there were vacant tables, many tables hosted groups of people mingling and engaging in laughter. She looked around to see if anyone had noticed her alone—if her father had noticed. No eyes met hers.

After sitting a moment in silence, she stood and discreetly

made her way across the floor, back to her father's table. She found an empty seat next to Harriet and reluctantly slouched in the chair. The only other empty seat was at the head of the table, in the direction of the Irving's alcove. *This must be Captain Kendall's chair*, she thought, not daring to occupy it. From where she now sat, she could look back across the room at her former table. She wondered if Harriet or anyone had noticed the scene created by Paden's father. *Probably not.* On her other side, sat Winifred. It was unusual for her maid to be joining her employer at the dinner table, but Winifred, no doubt, was content to consume a free First Class meal in exchange for her services rendered. *Her role as chaperone will benefit her quite well this week*, thought Grace. *It will be interesting to see how Winifred adjusts to genuine life back in England.*

Grace's father glanced across the table at his daughter. He smiled and nodded to her, acknowledging that she was welcome to sit, as she had done previously. One of the other table guests, whose name Grace had now forgotten, continued to tell a story about a survivor of the Titanic, and her father didn't interrupt to speak to Grace. Harriet turned to Grace with a disapproving frown, but manufactured a grin back at the man who spoke with a cigar in his right hand, and motioning in the air with his left hand.

"Imagine having to decide whether to save yourself by getting into a lifeboat, or to sacrifice to save another. It's simply ghastly to think about." He continued speaking with keen ears attuned to his voice, speaking of lifeboats, lifebelts, explosions. Grace shuddered at the thought of such a topic of conversation. She herself had understandably thought of the Titanic when she first arrived on deck and spoke with Paden. But, this was too deep. Too detailed. Too tragic. It was beyond distasteful for dinner dialogue.

Another voice filtered in. It belonged to an older woman to

Grace's left. "I heard that many people died before they drowned. Just from jumping ship and hitting the water. The cork vests snapped their necks like that," she said while cracking open a small, crisp bread stick with her hands.

Grace flinched with the sound, and then covered her forehead with her hand while adjusting her posture in her chair.

"Perhaps, we should strive to think more positively in our conversation this evening," spoke Grace's father, stealing a glance at Grace, then the party at the table. They seemed to understand his sensitivity towards Grace and the topic was swiftly changed.

"Any plans for a game of quoits on deck later, Mr. Bishop?" asked her father of a gentleman across the table.

"I'm afraid my aim is quite off these days," the man replied, "but I might be persuaded to a card game later in the Music Room."

Grace imagined the vacant Music Room that she had been in earlier. Her father had made the fleeting remark about her possibly playing the piano. It was probably stolen from his memory by now, and replaced with the gentle fluttering sound of cards being shuffled by skilled hands.

The conversation continued, although Grace did not adhere to joining in. Several waiters floated by the table, depositing plates of food. The food appeared so ornately prepared that she hardly recognized the dish as poultry. She began eating and was less than subtle at how hungry she was, cleaning her plate while others had barely lifted a utensil.

She raised her head from her place setting to sip a glass of water sitting in front of her. As she did so, she noticed a uniform, surfacing at the head of the table.

"Good evening gentlemen, ladies," greeted the man as he shuffled his chair behind himself to sit. As his head raised itself upright again, Grace was stunned. It was Paden's father. The very same man who tore into Paden. Yet, he seemed to have a pleasing disposition, all smiles and head nods to his guests at the table. His voice echoed Paden's English accent, but somewhat more sophisticated. "Captain Kendall sends his regrets this evening, folks. He so wanted to be here, but this being the first few hours out of port, I am hoping you understand."

"Is everything all right? We're not sinking are we?" spoke a horrid voice, followed by an equally disturbing cackle. It was Harriet.

What an embarrassment to Father, thought Grace in pity.

"Everything is just fine," he said reassuringly. "Why do you ask?" Mr. Thomas served an artificial smile.

Grace could tell he was not comfortable being the Captain's representative at the table. *Is he still bothered by his bout with Paden?* wondered Grace. *Or, is there something else about this man?*

After an awkward silence where Harriet was left defenceless in her questioning, Grace's father broke in. "Yes, well, not that we expect anything to be wrong. We were simply entertaining the connection between this liner and the…" he hesitated with a swallow, "the Titanic." Her father flashed a short, nervous smile, and shoved a forkful of food in his mouth, quickly chomping his teeth into the morsels of poultry.

"Connection?" queried Assistant Chief Steward Thomas with straight lips and eyebrows reaching down. He was starting to appear a little more like the man that Grace had encountered moments earlier at the other table. "I wasn't aware that there was any connection."

Mr. Bishop, the card player, spoke up. "I think what Mr. Hathaway means is that being aboard a liner such as this one…when you don't travel by ship that often…well, sometimes people cannot help but forge the association. But, I'm sure that someone of your sea experience would not worry about such things. You have probably sailed many a league without worry."

"Indeed," returned Mr. Thomas. A hesitation occurred. A plate of food was placed in front of him. He peered around the table and realized that everyone had started to consume the meal. Picking up his fork, he shovelled a bite in. In his appearance, Mr. Thomas was dressed like a First Class steward, wearing a white, double-breasted tunic with decorative cording on the end of his sleeves near his hands. However, in his manner, he revealed a lack of refinement like that of Paden. Perhaps this was why he seemed uncomfortable with dining in the captain's place. He abruptly clanked his fork and knife onto his plate and resumed speaking, with his first few words being masked behind his chewing of poultry and potatoes. "There is hardly any resemblance to our tragic counterpart. I'm sure you would find, if you were to investigate further and be duly educated, that we are in a far better position than those on the Titanic, to say the least."

"Let us hope so," blurted Winifred. She appeared to remember her place and submissively lowered her head amidst raised eyebrows at the table, particularly those of Harriet.

"Much planning went into the crafting and building of this ship. From the first sketches in 1904, to her completion and maiden voyage in 1906. She's perfectly fitted and smoothly operational on all eight decks. She's been sailing some eight years now. That alone, far exceeds the Titanic's lifetime. While she may not be as luxurious as the Titanic, she holds her own. Modern electric lights. A ventilation and heating system that allows for a change of air in every compartment every ten minutes."

"Safety features?" asked Grace's father. Grace wondered if he were indulging the steward, so that the man could successfully justify his position. Perhaps her father felt awkward about his table's comments, and was helping the man save face—the man who was saving his captain from the burden of defending his ship during dinner, when more important duties were being executed.

"As I am sure you are all fully aware," spoke Mr. Thomas, glancing around the table, "most of the casualties surrounding the Titanic disaster came about from a deficiency of lifeboats. You may have noticed as you walked the Upper Promenade Deck, that we have many said boats. We also have a deck, appropriately named 'Boat Deck' for the simple reason that it houses an abundance of lifeboats. Since the Titanic disaster, more lifeboats have been outfitted. We have a number of steel boats, as well as collapsible Berthon boats. We have recently added some more wood ones, as well. Not to mention all the lifebelts on board."

The table occupants simply stared, remaining silent.

Mr. Thomas gave less hesitation now, as before. He remembered his pitch, and continued on. "We have navigational telephones, and wireless communication. Eleven watertight compartments, as well as watertight doors, ensure that we can stay afloat in the event we take on water. Daily drills ensure that our crew successfully operate the gears needed to close these doors. Captain Kendall has the crew running a variety of drills and inspections on safety equipment from fire extinguishers to emergency oil lamps in the passageways. So, as you can figure it, many hours of planning, preparing, and executing safety precautions have been sacrificed. This is the Empress of Ireland—not the Titanic."

With that comment, Mr. Thomas resumed his meal with repeated utensil action. It was as though he was an educated lawyer that fought a mighty court battle, and now rested his case. He had represented his ship well, and had done his duty for his client, the captain, and his crew. Grace admired his loyalty and was starting to see him as less of a monster than when she had met him across the room, only moments earlier.

For the first time in minutes, there was a lull in the conversation. Grace once again noticed the musicians were still playing. A mischievous melody emerged. One that Grace immediately recognized. She had played it on the piano for one of her lessons, some time ago. She couldn't quite remember its title. *Marionette something. March of the…Funeral March of a Marionette, by Gunoud. That was it,* she remembered. She was internally amused as she realized the implications of the haunting, but playful melody in light of the previous conversation topic—the Titanic—a conversation that was in itself, haunting, yet playfully mishandled by the dinner guests.

Moments passed while quiet conversation resumed between couples at the table. Just as everyone seemed to be quite finished the main course, a steward in a tunic matching that of Mr. Thomas, approached the table and whispered into Mr. Thomas' ear.

"Thank you," he said, lifting his white cloth table napkin off his lap and placing it beside his plate, the Canadian Pacific logo clearly readable. "Mr. Hathaway," he said, looking at Grace's father. "That matter of business that you wanted to take care of is now ready. At your convenience, of course."

"Now will be adequate. It shan't take a moment."

"Very well," returned Mr. Thomas, rising and pulling down the bottom of his tunic.

"My dear," spoke Grace's father to Harriet. "Will you be all right? I shall be back momentarily."

Harriet gave a quick nod and an 'if you must' expression, and glanced at her watch.

"Grace," spoke her father again.

Grace was surprised that he would acknowledge her, since he had left her alone already, without second thought.

"Would you like to accompany me to the purser's office? I promise to have you back in time for dessert."

Grace was ready to get out of the Dining Saloon. "Very well." In fact, it would be the first time she would be alone with her father on this trip, apart from the few spare moments in their room upon arrival.

"Right this way, Mr Hathaway," spoke Mr. Thomas, as he walked ahead of Grace and her father, away from the table and towards the piano. A quick right and Grace would be led out into the hall. The captain's assistant chief steward motioned for Grace and her father to turn right, once clearing the dining saloon doors. She saw two men in ship's uniform standing at the doorway of a room just shy of the gangway doors through which she had first entered upon boarding the ship. A sign on the door read, "Purser's Office". The two men, each with broad shoulders, correct upright posture and a certain uncompromising stare gave Grace the impression that they were guarding Buckingham Palace. *This must be where the silver is being kept*, she surmised.

The two men each saluted Mr. Thomas, but remained firm in their disposition. He reciprocated the salute and then used a set of jingling keys to open the door. Once inside, he shut the door behind Grace and her father and locked it with the key again.

"Your safe is here, sir. I trust you will be relieved to see that everything is in order."

Grace knew of that which he spoke. Her father was quite anxious about his mine's silver bars the entire trip. From the ride in the motorcar, to the train station in Toronto. Then, every waking moment on the train, Grace had listened to her father worry. He spoke of how the silver bars arrived the day before by train. Hired police were to see to its safe arrival aboard the Empress. Then, at all times, two handpicked crewmen guarded it. It was shipped in its own special safe, and the safe was to be transported aboard and placed in the purser's office for safe keeping, next to the ship's main safe. Grace was certain that her father would not rest until he saw to its final resting place in London. If the bars went missing, he would certainly have a scandal that would ruin any future plans of success in London.

"Pardon me, Grace," spoke her father as he moved past her to get to the black combination safe. Her father put his hands on the palm-sized dial and began spinning it in clockwise and counter-clockwise directions. It was three or four spins in total, and then the safe handle was cranked. Grace heard a metal 'click' as he pulled the door slightly open. She could only grasp a slight glimpse of the contents. Inside, she saw partial glimmers of the office's electric ceiling light, being reflected off the shiny bars. The bars were housed in many stacks—eight or ten high, and who knows how many wide. He pulled out a piece of paper and examined it momentarily. "The shipping label?" asked Mr. Thomas.

"Yes, sir. As you can see, they are all accounted for," returned the steward.

"Very well. I'm going to place some cash from my wallet in the safe. Will I be able to retrieve it as often as I require?"

"Of course, sir. You are the only one who knows the combination. It will be safe, for certain."

Grace witnessed her father take a large fold of bills from his wallet and place it in the safe on top of the bars. He wasted no time in closing the iron door, pulling the handle, and spinning the combination knob. He was being much more careful with things than when he first lost his wallet upon coming aboard. Grace couldn't help but be amused by the large safe. If anyone wanted to steal the silver, they would have a difficult time moving the bars. They were so...unaccommodating to the average pickpocket. The safe didn't appear to be bolted down, but that would be redundant as it was sure to weigh enough for an army of men to carry. All this, in addition to the two thugs posted outside the room caused Grace to be certain that her father's cash and the mine's bars would be quite safe.

Upon exiting the room, Grace, her father, and Mr. Thomas, began to make their way back towards the Dining Saloon. Before coming to the room's main doors, Grace noticed Mr. Steele walking down the staircase.

"Ah, Mr. Steele," spoke Paden's father.

"Yes, sir," came the reply as crewman Steele approached the small party.

"Mr. Steele will be overseeing operations on Shelter Deck, as well as Upper and Lower Promenade Decks. If you should need anything, or wish to get into the safe, he is the man to approach…or myself, of course."

"Mr. Steele," spoke her father, accompanied by a nod of his head.

"I shall keep a keen watch on things for you sir. Although, it's not like your investment isn't secure anyway. There is no where for a would-be-thief to go on the ship, except overboard into the sea," he spoke with a confident chuckle. "I make it my business to be privy to every detail aboard this ship. You can count on me."

"Please excuse us for a moment," spoke Mr. Thomas to Grace and her father, as the two men stepped aside a few feet. "Mr. Steele," spoke Mr. Thomas, in a quiet, but harsh tone that Grace could still make out. "Your confidence in your abilities is reassuring, but you mustn't be overly confident. If anything happens to that silver, I shall hold you personally responsible. Do we have an understanding?"

Grace noticed Mr. Steele's throat 'gulp' as he returned comments to Thomas. He spoke quieter than Thomas and she couldn't make out his words. She was beginning to feel that Mr. Steele was attempting to win favours with her father. He seemed to be overdoing his loyalty routine. She wondered if he were too boastful about himself and his work. This belief would coincide with her observations of his condescending attitude towards Paden.

"I should get back to my dinner guests," spoke Mr. Thomas, returning with a smile to Grace and her father, and a salute to Mr. Steele.

Mr. Steele flagged his salute and turned to the remaining two. "Good evening," he said, and turned back towards the staircase and marched up.

"Well, Grace," spoke her father. "Shall we see about dessert?" he said, holding out his arm for her to take.

Now that she had escaped the high society of the First Class Dining Saloon, she wondered if she could avoid going back. "Father, I have somewhat of a pain in my head. Would you be offended if I return to our room? I haven't quite recovered from all the travelling as of yet."

Her father looked into her eyes and didn't respond immediately. It was as though he were trying to figure her motives. After a brief pause, he responded. "Yes, of course, Grace. Whatever you like. These past few days...months, really, have been an adjustment for you."

An adjustment. An adjust—that's an understatement, she thought.

"Do take care of yourself. I will probably be out entertaining Harriet, or sitting with some of the gentlemen in the First Class Café or Music Saloon. Do not feel as though you have to wait up for me."

Grace nodded, and her father kissed her forehead. She turned towards the staircase and he disappeared into the Dining Saloon doorway. As she climbed the two stories up the grand staircase that would lead her back to her room, she was surprised at how empty the Upper Promenade seemed. Everyone was dining downstairs. Grace turned left at the top of the stairs, headed past

Harriet and Winifred's room, unconcerned about an encounter with Harriet who remained two decks down, making silly remarks to the table host.

Cutting through the first door of the Music Room that would lead to her room, Grace was surprised the room was empty. She imagined that there would be some early occupants. No doubt, some would arrive soon, as dinner had almost come to full fruition. She stepped further towards the rear door. About to pass through, she glanced back at the empty piano stool. Her family had once owned a grand piano like that sitting before her. When her mother died, it was given to her Aunt Nona, even though her aunt didn't play. It was one of the few possessions from Grace's former life that wasn't sold off. She would never touch its ivory keys again.

She slipped out of the room and put her book inside her room, setting it on her luggage. *It would be nice to play that piano...but, what if someone were to come?* She found her feet moving back into the Music Room. *They wouldn't approve of a 'child' playing*, thought Grace with a scowl in remembrance of Harriet's unkind remarks earlier. *A child. Can a child play like this?* she thought defiantly as she stormed the piano, lifted its lid, and pounded out the opening measures of Dvorak's "Going Home" from "The New World Symphony."

As she firmly progressed through each rich chord, hearing them before her fingers made tangible contact, she thought of the teachings of her piano teacher, Mrs. Francis. She taught Grace that one could not grasp the meaning of the music simply by pressing the right keys. One had to know the motivations and the message. She approached the end of the main melody, but added arpeggios to the final chord, entering into a reprise. As the music rang off the dome ceiling back to her ears, she thought of Dvorak composing this song, a Czech composer living in America, longing for memories of his homeland. How she could identify with him now. As she approached the final chord, she launched into her own melody, and added chords that she knew, as a musician, would work well together. Her new improvised melody came natural to her; it had a tone of sadness, yet resolve. It depicted mourning, yet predicted a positive ending. She had found the tune, and repeated it several times so that she wouldn't forget it, giving it support with the chords from her left hand. She played until—

"Uh…I'm sorry…I didn't mean—" spoke a voice.

Grace pried her hands off the keys. Her eyes didn't lift up from the piano, but she recognized the voice as Paden's. "I am the one who is sorry. I shouldn't be touching the piano. There was no one here, so I—"

"It's all right. It's only me—not that bloke, Steele. You can do what you like. S'fine by me," he said shrugging his shoulders.

"What are you doing here? Shouldn't you be doing what your father told you? You know, ship's business and all?"

He smiled. "I have a real knack for not doing what I'm s'posed to."

"That's becoming apparent," she said, returning the smile.

"That was a beautiful tune you were playing. What is it called?"

"I suppose you could call it, 'Saving Grace,'" she said, not expecting him to understand.

"That's a funny title for someone who doesn't need savin'."

"Yes," she acknowledged, "I suppose you're right."

"Seriously, though. Who wrote it?" he persisted.

"Well, the last bit I was playing…it was just an improvisation." Grace noticed that Paden wore a blank expression. Perhaps he didn't know the meaning of the word. She clarified. "I just made it up."

"Can you make something else up for me?" he asked.

"No. I'm not very good at writing my own music. But, I could play some Dvorak for you."

"Why would I want to hear from someone I've never heard of before? I want you to play something of Grace."

"No, I can't."

"Please," he insisted.

"The answer is 'NO'," she spoke harshly, slamming the lid shut on the piano. Paden's eyes widened and she realized she had been rude. She quickly regained her composure. "I'm sorry. I guess I'm fatiqued. It has been too long of a day to get my brain working in that way."

"Yes, well, I came looking for you. I felt poorly about the dinner table incident. You know, with my father. What say I take you on a grand tour of the ship? Show you the ins and outs?"

Grace hesitated. She was feeling somewhat weary, yet Paden was feeding her a youthful spirit that was lacking in her company two decks below. "I don't know. My father might not approve. Harriet—she would definitely not approve," spoke Grace with a slight grin and a shake of her head.

"That's all the more reason to do it then, isn't it?" came the reply.

Grace's mind was inadvertently stolen from the room. *That's all the more reason to do it then*, she thought as she remembered her cousin Andrew's words.

"Let's go to the falls," he insisted.

Grace had always known that she was not a strong enough swimmer to go there, and that it was dangerously deep. Andrew was visiting town with her aunt. He knew their rules, but he had too much confidence.

"Mother would never approve," she insisted.

"That's all the more reason to do it then," he said.

"So what ya' think?" asked Paden. "Grace? Ya' with me?"

Grace shook her head rapidly to snap out of her past. She sobered up to reply, "I'm sorry. I was a bit distracted. Please. I appreciate the kindness, but I must be getting to my room. I'm quite spent. Perhaps another—"

"Grace," spoke Paden with a straight tone. His smile had gone as he lifted Grace from the piano bench and grasped her arm firmly. "Look. You 'ave to come with me. I 'ave some important information for you regarding your father and the silver."

The First Class Music Room

Chapter 5

"The silver?" asked an astonished Grace. "What business have you with my father's silver?"

"Oh, so it belongs to your father now, does it?"

Grace shook her head. "My father's. The mine's. I don't care whose it is. What important information do you have?"

Grace thought Paden was about to utter an answer when voices were heard murmuring outside the room. Paden looked towards the door, then back at Grace. "Look. We 'ave to talk about this in private. There are things that you are not privy to on this ship. Things that could get me into deep water if I told you."

"Don't worry, Paden. I'm not going to kill the messenger."

"Huh?" he asked.

"Sophocles. Never mind. Is someone going to—" she started but was silenced by Paden's hand over her mouth.

"Here, let's go back this way," he said, taking her by the arm and escorting her to the forward door of the Music Room, past Harriet and Winifred's room, and towards the hallway of the staircase. Several passengers were making their way up the staircase from the Lower Promenade Deck as Paden moved away from the staircase towards a set of double doors that led to the deck outside.

"Where are we going?" asked Grace as she felt the cool breeze being tossed against her face. It was darker now and she was seeing shadows, rather than people. There were only a couple of silhouettes outside on the starboard deck. Most people were wise enough to stay indoors. It was too dark for Grace to see her watch, but she surmised that it must be close to 8:30.

"Watch your step," cautioned Paden as he turned right, and began climbing a set of stairs. Grace followed, grasping the handrail carefully and obediently, without question. It was too breezy to question at this point, for she wanted to hear clearly, every word Paden would speak about her father. She could wait another few moments until they secured a quiet solace.

They topped the stairs and moved up deck, towards the bow of the ship, having passed the forward funnel. Grace remembered the shaft for the forward funnel in the Dining Saloon and figured they were approaching the roof above the main staircase. Just past the forward funnel, Paden stopped at a door that read, "Officer's Quarters". She thought it curious that he should stop here. It wasn't any degree quieter. The waves, rhythmically pounding the side of the ship, echoed up its massive hull and over the deck into Grace's ears. Although they had to be many stories below, the waves pulsed as though they would topple directly over her.

Starting to feel uncomfortable in the cold shadowy night, Grace opened dialogue once again. "Why have you brought me here, Paden?"

"There are a few things I need to tell you, but it would be easier to show you," he returned, his face wearing some dim yellow light that filtered through the door's porthole window.

"Get to the point. It's cold out here," she said shivering, and crossing her arms while she rubbed her hands up and down over them. She found it necessary to raise her voice above the waves, as she had to strain to hear Paden. Hopefully, he would echo the same tone.

"All right," he said impatiently and emphatically. "There's a plan to steal your father's silver."

"The mine's silver?" she asked, not intending on correcting Paden.

"Your father's silver. The mine's silver. Whoever owns the silver. It doesn't much matter. If you don't listen to me, the only people owning those silver bars will be a long ways from your father or his mine."

"How do you know this?" she asked sceptically.

"I told you. I'm free to travel this ship. I know it in and out. I've been to places that even the cap'n doesn't know exist. I have an ear to her crew, too. They've been aware of your father's coming aboard for days by way of the mine's shipping manifests. They even watched the silver get loaded yesterday. It's not a matter of whether the silver will be taken, but when it will be taken."

"This is all difficult to believe. I can't believe that someone aboard this ship could come up with such a plan. I mean, where would they hide the silver? There's nowhere to go. I'm sure missing silver would be easily traced. No one would be permitted off the ship until it was found. I think you have been misled."

Paden was obviously uptight, as his face moved closer to Grace's. "There are things that I would like to show you, but we don't have the luxury of time."

"Good evening, Paden," came a voice from behind Grace in the darkness. It startled her as it broke the sound of the waves.

"Evenin' Murphy," returned Paden to another young ship's officer in uniform and cap. "Workin' tonight?" asked Paden.

"Yeah. Just finishing. I just have to go to the bridge and the chart room. Test the fire extinguishers. You never know when a fire might erupt on the bridge, eh?" he said with a wink and a quick jerk of his head sideways.

Grace felt that the delivery of the last comment was meant as though he and Paden shared a common secret. They both nodded together in agreement. She felt as though she missed something in their meaning.

"The question is: are YOU working this evening?" asked the man, probably about eighteen years old, as he looked at Grace and smiled.

"You could say that, Murph'. Just showin' the lady the ship, ya' know."

"Yeah, I know. Eh, don't let Steele catch you taking the lady to restricted areas. He's out on the watch. Looking to bust any crew members with as much as an untied shoelace."

Paden calmly laughed. "All right," he said with a smile, "thanks for the storm warning."

"Enjoy the tour, Miss." Crewman Murphy entered the door next to Paden and disappeared down the hallway that was visible to Grace beyond the porthole.

"Should we go now?" asked Grace.

"No, don't worry 'bout him. He's all right. My mate. Besides, I need to show you the bridge."

"I don't think that would be a good idea," protested Grace. "I'm not supposed—"

"Relax, Grace. I won't take you right in. Don't want to get Father into it with the cap'n. I just want you to catch a glimpse."

Paden motioned for Grace to follow as he moved past the door to the crew quarters and past another door. He shifted slightly to the right to negotiate his way around some kind of metal island structure on deck. Once around its shadowy hull, Grace could see five dimly lit rectangular bridge windows facing the bow. She looked down at the bow to see silhouettes of riggings, masts, and other unrecognizable dark shapes. As she cowered away from the view of the bridge windows, for fear of getting herself, or Paden, into trouble from the bridge crew, she noticed that the bridge lighting was low. *Must be rigged for night viewing*, she thought. *The crew must have good night eyes, in order to pierce the darkness of the water ahead.*

"That, there's the cap'n," spoke Paden raising his head to one window, while keeping his hands warm in both front pockets of his trousers. Grace noticed that Paden was able to speak in softer tones, as they stood in the solace of the forward bridge wall, sheltering them from the strong wind at the side of the ship.

Grace moved closer and struggled to see inside the bridge windows. Lighting was sufficient enough to see a man who seemed in his early forties, for he looked approximately the same age as her father. He wore a dark, double-breasted tunic like other crew, a necktie, and carried a white and black cap under his arm. He stood back from another officer who was positioned at what Paden described as the ship's wheelhouse.

Grace didn't understand what all the equipment was for, but recognized the ship's wheel, exactly as she imagined it. A spoked wheel with knob-like handles protruding—enough for a person to grab hold and spin around. She trusted that the ship's crew, including her captain, knew what they were doing. She was taken aback at the captain, who she expected to be an old man with a greying beard, and a monocle in one eye. The average fisherman-at-sea look, like one would read about in stories. This man appeared strong. Capable. In the prime of his life. Yet he stood off at a distance from the wheelhouse.

"The cap'n's lettin' the pilot do the work right now. Until we get out of the river," explained Paden, once again motioning with his head towards the wheelhouse. "Mr. Bernier is steering us out to sea. He'll guide us 'round other ships that might pass, keeping us on course. Then we'll drop him at Father Point, sometime after our mail drop in Rimouski. It'll all be on the cap'n then."

Grace thought of the implications of what Paden was saying. The cap'n of the ship, allowing someone else to command, if only for a short while. How she wished she had a pilot to guide her. Steer her on the proper course. Adjust her heading when necessary. At this point, she had her own "Father Point". Only, she didn't feel comfortable with her father in command. Like the captain, she had been standing back, entrusting her life in his command. *Can I break command? Control my own destiny? Is it too late?* she wondered.

Grace realized that she was daydreaming, and focused her gaze on the bridge officers again. She noticed another person enter the room. It was crewman Murphy, carrying a fire extinguisher. He looked towards Grace and Paden, as though he could see them. Grace was becoming perplexed at why she was there. Why had Paden brought her? While the engulfing brisk air movement had subsided directly in the shelter of the bridge wall, Grace wanted to go back inside the ship.

"What did you bring me here to tell me?" she asked Paden, sounding an air of frustration.

"It's not what I wanted to tell you here. It's what I wanted to show you."

Grace was still confused. "What do you mean? The bridge? The captain? What are you getting at?"

"Listen, Grace. The best way I can explain this to you, is to show it to you. There are a few places I need to take you first. You 'ave to trust me. Give me an hour of your time, and all will be made clear. I need to take you back inside, to our next stop."

"Our next stop? You mean on the 'let's make Grace a fool' tour? You're not giving me any answers. Only more questions."

"Grace, if you are at all concerned about your father and the fortune entrusted to him, then I suggest you give me a short bit of your time. All will be clear in the end."

Grace shook her head in disagreement. She had a mind to say 'Good evening' and head off to bed. She was feeling as though she had reached the limits of her 'cold threshold' and had to go inside. Since returning indoors was Paden's intention, as part of the next stop on his bewildering walking tour, she agreed to continue with him for the time being.

"Lead on," she said.

Turning the corner around the bridge wall, heading back down the Boat Deck, Grace was hit with an invisible wall that pulled her hair out of her bun, and her dress in multiple directions. She had to fight to keep her legs in forward movement as she held her hair out of her face.

Moments later, Paden and Grace made contact with the same stairs that they had ascended moments earlier. First Grace, followed by Paden. As Grace set foot on the Lower Promenade Deck, she turned away from the stairs, only to hear a cry from behind.

"Blimy!" shouted Paden as he attempted to pick himself off the wooden deck. He was sprawled on his hands and knees.

"Are you all right?" asked Grace.

"What a stupid thing to do!" he exclaimed in disgust. "I twisted me' ankle. I think it could be broken."

"Are you sure?" asked Grace. Her thoughts returned to the riverside with Andrew. "Andrew, we have to get back. We're not supposed to swim here," she had insisted.

"I can't," Andrew said jesting. "I twisted my ankle. I can't make it back. I guess we'll have to stay," he said laughing and sitting on the riverbank. Once his shoes were fully removed, he crawled on his hands and knees and reached out his hand in a continued charade. "Help me up."

"Stop the games, Andrew," Grace had insisted.

"What games? Help me up."

She reached to pull him up, only to find herself pulled into his deceit and into the frigid lake water. He had fooled her sure enough. If she hadn't been wearing her bathing costume, she certainly would have left him alone in the water.

"I'm not sure if it's broke," said Paden. But, it hurts something awful. I need to get to the ship's hospital. Get the doctor to check it out."

"Where's that?" asked Grace, her mind focused again on Paden.

"It's below. On Shelter Deck. Near the stern. Take my hand."

Grace reached down and pulled Paden up. He was surprisingly heavy for a pole of a lad, with Grace not being that strong in stature.

"I'll lead and you support," said Paden, wrapping his arm around Grace, suspending his left knee in the air, and hobbling in the direction of the ship's stern. They continued down the breezy deck, past room windows, some lit, some dark. Eventually, they made it to a staircase going down to the utmost stern of the ship on Lower Promenade Deck. Grace remembered this set of stairs from earlier on when she caught a glimpse of Paden being berated by the stranger behind the capsized lifeboat. The very same lifeboat that she was heading towards.

"Down 'ere," spoke Paden in a broken voice of pain. He gestured with his head for Grace to turn down a staircase that would lead them back to Shelter Deck. They would navigate to the same deck where Grace ate dinner, but she had not been this far back on the ship. It was unexplored territory and she was unaware of her surroundings. Another turn from the bottom of the staircase to the rear of the ship's deck. A door leading inside. They were in. Out of the cold.

"Just ahead," directed Paden. Grace assisted Paden through a medical room. "This is the women's hospital. Just through 'ere to the men's." She continued with him to another door. Paden knocked, but then ushered his way in, taking Grace with him.

"Yes," sounded a voice. A man wearing a long white coat turned around from some paperwork at a work desk. "What do we have here?"

"A twisted ankle. Possibly a break," spoke Grace first. She was surprised that the doctor appeared as a young man, no facial wrinkles, clean-shaven and handsome. *If a real emergency broke out on the ship, would he know what to do?* wondered Grace.

"Sit him here," said the doctor, directing Grace and Paden to a bed. "Let's have a look at it." He unrolled Paden's right leg cuff, and gently pulled away his black sock. "Well, there doesn't appear to be any swelling. How does it feel when I do this?" he asked, manoeuvring the ankle from side to side.

"Stop!" cried Paden. "That's awful!"

Grace stood back away from the two, allowing the doctor to conduct his examination. She looked around the room. She noticed a certificate on the wall. Dr. James Frederick Grant. A degree from McGill University. Her suspicions were put to rest. *He's a real doctor.* She scanned the small room for other signs of medical practice. Various metal instruments lay neatly out on a sterile cloth. A cabinet with a windowed door, housing various bottles and potions. She focused back on Paden and the doctor.

"Try standing for me. Mr. Thomas, isn't it?"

"Yes, that's right."

"I understand your father was recently promoted. What does he think of the new captain? Gently. Go easy at first," he said helping Paden stand firmly.

"Real nasty," said Paden.

"The captain?"

"Huh? No, I mean the ankle. Do you have anything for the pain, doctor?"

"Well, as I have indicated, there doesn't appear to be any swelling. If you are experiencing pain, it will be short-lived, I believe."

"Doc," spoke Paden. "I 'ave to get a fair rest this evening. I have my duties to perform tomorrow. The cap'n's new assistant chief steward will not like it if I'm unfit for duty. Know what I mean?"

The doctor gazed into Paden's eyes and appeared to have correctly interpreted Paden's concern with reference to his father. "Very well. Take two of these and you will sleep," spoke the man, giving Paden two red pills in an otherwise empty, clear container.

"How often can I take them? Can I have more?"

"You won't know what hit you after the first two." He looked back at Paden who gave a desperate face, no hint of contentment. "But, I suppose I could give you a few more, just in case. He reached into the medicine cabinet, rattled another bottle, and placed four more of the red pills into the clear container.

"Thanks, Doc," spoke Paden, now with a smile on his face.

He nodded in return. "You will steer him towards the crew quarters, will you?" asked the doctor of Grace.

"Yes, of course. Thank you." Grace shouldered Paden's weight again and assisted him out the door. For some reason, he seemed a little lighter and less burdensome. *Perhaps the pain is starting to subside*, she thought. *If there was any pain to begin with.*

Making their way outside again through the hospital door on the port side, Grace spoke hardly a word to Paden. She simply followed his lead. They moved forward up the deck to a Second Class entrance, leading into a hallway that divided the Second Class Social Hall towards the stern, and the Second Class Dining Saloon towards the bow.

"Let's cut through 'ere," said Paden, nodding towards the door leading into the Dining Saloon.

Grace observed that the room itself did not seem as elegant as the First Class Dining Saloon, having less sculpturing and duller furniture, but it was satisfactory. She saw that a number of passengers were still seated, enjoying dessert and beverages. Many of these passengers wore uniforms. Not ship uniforms, but Salvation Army uniforms. As she led Paden across the floor, there were a few smiles from the curious onlookers.

Once completing the awkward public jaunt through the Dining Saloon, they proceeded through another set of doors. These doors led to another passageway that covered across the width of the ship.

Every step of the way, Grace contemplated the situation she was in. *Why am I doing this?* she asked herself. *I should go to bed. Father is probably looking for me. Who are these supposed crewmen that are looking to steal the silver? Could the doctor be one? Is that why we had a sudden visit to the hospital? And Murphy? What was that about? The whole thing with the fire extinguisher.* Grace was ready to drop Paden here in the passageway. *Enough is enough.*

"Look Paden—"

"Paden," spoke a voice behind Grace. She turned to see another crewman about Paden's age, wearing white galley clothes, apron and all. He was oriental and he donned a white, tiny hat that hugged his head, making him look like a baker-in-training. Had Grace met him under less frustrating circumstances, she might have burst out laughing at him as he smiled at her with flour on the tip of his nose.

"Eddie," nodded Paden to his friend. He returned a glance to Grace. "This is Edmund. We call him 'Fast Eddie'."

"Fast Eddie?" asked Grace. "Never mind," she continued, shaking her head.

"If you need something done," said Paden, "Eddie's the one to get it done for you—lightning fastest. Eddie, did you take care of those arrangements that I asked for?"

"All's taken care of Pade'," spoke Eddie. He bore a rich smile and a friendly spirit.

"Well done, Eddie," returned Paden. "Now, Grace, there is one more thing that I need to ask of you before we go any further. It's going to require that you trust me."

"Trust you? I've only made your acquaintance a short while ago. I hardly know you. And every corner I allow you to take me deeper into the heart of this ship, we meet up with strangers that either can't tolerate you, or are your mates." Grace turned to Eddie who was watching the conversation unfold as they stood there in the passageway, just the three of them.

"Sorry, Eddie, but this is too fast for me. I neither know you, nor trust you."

"Don't worry about Eddie," reassured Paden. "I've known him for weeks."

"Weeks?" spoke Grace, astonished. Paden seemed to think that 'weeks' was sufficient enough to build relationships between people. She had spent her entire lifetime knowing her father, and now their father-daughter relationship seemed to be crumbling. She knew and trusted her cousin, Andrew, for a long time, yet he persuaded her to trust his misguided judgment, causing him to drown. Trust takes a long time to forge, yet so quickly becomes unravelled. For some reason, though, she felt as though these young men meant her no harm. *Pastry boy here, hardly looks as though he could hurt anyone,* she thought. *And Paden. He seems to have his enemies, but Murphy and Eddie are loyal enough to him.*

Grace seemed content enough to trust the two for the time being. "What do you need from me?" she asked resolutely.

Paden stepped aside to show Grace a silver metal cart on

wheels. It had several dishes on top, and sliding panel doors on the side. "We need to take you inside the galley, but we can't allow you to be seen. It would arouse too much attention. We need you to—"

"Wait a minute," interjected Grace. "If you think that I'm climbing into that thing to hide, then you are mistaken." She looked at both of them.

Eddie spoke up. "It's all right, Miss, see." He opened the panels on the side. Fittings for a metal shelf appeared to have been removed, allowing the cavity to house a small person, and a big deception. "We'll even leave it open a crack for you to see."

"What is the purpose of this?" she demanded.

"Grace," spoke Paden in a calm voice as he moved close to her. "Everything I told you about your father's silver. All your questions. I can answer once we are beyond these doors. You 'ave to trust me, just a little further. Please."

Grace sighed. "What are you doing, Grace?" she said to herself as she hiked her dress above her boots, tilted her head, and gave her arm to Paden as she climbed down into the cart. Her boots gave an echoing 'boom' inside the small hull. The same noise occurred when she pushed her back against the flimsy wall. She noticed that there were several canvas bags inside to sit on. She was able to grab hold of one to read a label on it. "Royal Mail".

Eddie began to slide the door closed on Grace. Just before she was covered in darkness, Paden poked his face under the tiny covering inside the steel structure. "Thanks, Grace. For trusting me."

Grace nodded and smiled. As the door shut further, she put her fingers in the way to permit a fragment of light and vision. She wanted to see what the two were up to. She felt the wheels, under her feet, rumble slightly. She saw the passageway door, then she was in another room. The galley. Voices could be heard. Male and female. White outfits, like Eddie's. The floor had black and white squares in a tessellating pattern. She noticed a shelf across from her that housed many white coffee mugs, bearing the "Canadian Pacific" logo. Looking up, she noticed many of the same mugs, as well as other glasses, hanging down from the ceiling. The ceiling looked remarkably different from anywhere else on the ship. No fancy mouldings, wood, or paint. Simply steel plates and rivets. Several pipes intersected and travelled the length of the ceiling. It was difficult to determine visual perception from the inside of the cart, but the ceiling appeared to be lower than in other places on the ship.

She was taken aback at how the inner workings of the ship, this area where most passengers would never see, seemed less artificial. The galley separated the First Class Dining Saloon, with all its fancy trimmings, from the Second Class Dining Saloon, which was more simplistic. Somewhere on this ship, there would be a Third Class Dining Saloon. Yet, the galley represented commonality. Here, at the heart of the Shelter Deck, there was no distinction between classes. No attempt of deception. The arteries leaving the galley were the same, but were masked in a skin of disguise for those more privileged in First Class, with their fancy whipped desserts, elegant table napkins, and fine dishes. If only all passengers could see the galley, and realize that there was neutral ground.

Grace felt the cart make several turns and she had to place her hands against the sides so that she wouldn't tip over and cause more noise on the steel walls. She listened to Paden and Eddie speaking to other crewmembers. Only broken fragments.

"Excuse me. Right then. 'Ow are ya'?" and others that seemed to suggest they were trying not to engage the crew, too much, but wanted to get around them.

Grace began feeling warmth inside the box. She thought she must be passing an oven or steamer, and that, in combination with the lack of fresh air entering her chamber, caused her to want to slide the door open in relief. The cart stopped briefly and she suspected she might be able to get out. She pulled the door open slightly, but it slammed on her fingers.

"Just a bit longer," she heard Paden's muffled voice.

Grace soaked her injured finger in her mouth, and winced in pain. *That Paden. He is in for it, now*, she thought. The cart stopped and a noise was heard that sounded like a door closing. Grace was out of breath. The lack of air in the box, as well as her air passageway being blocked by her hunched sitting position caused her to grab the edge of the metal door, fling it open, and fall out.

"Easy," spoke Paden, lifting Grace from the floor.

"Where are we?" insisted Grace. She stood with Paden and Eddie in a confined square space with the cart. There was no room for either to move. She looked up and around. "I didn't realize there were lifts aboard this ship," she said.

"This is the only one, Miss," spoke Eddie. "It's a service lift."

Grace looked down at the cart. The mugs and dishes that once sat on top, had been replaced by several dessert cakes and whipped delights. She was puzzled. "What's all this?"

"Dessert," answered Paden with a stolen smile to Eddie.

Grace looked at both of them. "That's it? You smuggled me into the galley to watch you steal sweets? I think I'm losing my mind," she said, burying her forehead into her hands.

"No Grace," spoke Paden, "the desserts are just another thing I 'ave to take care of. My main purpose is to do what I said I'd do. Show you what you need to know."

The lift bounced to a halt and Eddie opened the door. Paden and Eddie filed out, pulled the cart out, and Paden took Grace's hand to lead her along. She immediately looked around, wondering where she was. Nothing looked familiar. No furniture, or windows. No mahogany doors or stain-glass windows. She was in the inner workings of the ship. Steel walls and pipes surrounded her.

"We're on Lower Deck," spoke Paden. "This stays here for now," he said, pushing the cart back into the lift. "Let's move, through here."

Grace, for the first time since following Paden, was genuinely scared. She didn't have any idea where she was. If something ill happened to her, no one would know where to find her. She followed Paden through passages, left and right turns, around coal and cargo, and past several filthy crewmen, in one-piece outfits, who were shovelling near furnaces in offshoot hallways. With coal at their feet, they mindlessly shovelled away.

"We're here," informed Paden as he led her into a massive opening for a room. Grace looked up and noticed that the opening apparently housed a vertical watertight door. The room itself appeared several decks high, and contained two monstrous machine structures.

This must be the engine room, she thought. *But it is difficult to think. So loud. So overwhelming.* She looked above at the metal structures. Parts moved back and forth, gushing, swishing, and pounding. Other workmen wandered around various walkways surrounding the engine, but none seemed concerned by anything but their own duties.

"Welcome to the heart of the ship," yelled Paden above the noise.

Grace looked at Paden, then at Eddie. She wasn't certain about them anymore. She wasn't certain about anything anymore. She tried to contain her panic as she spoke. "I want to leave now, Paden. Take me back."

"But, Grace," he insisted.

"No, take me back to my father!" she shouted. "You said you were going to show me what I needed to know."

"But, I have Grace. I have shown you everything you need to know. I have shown you exactly how your father's silver will be taken."

Grace stood back in bewilderment. "What are you talking about?" she said, eyes wide open, and wandering from side to side.

"Let us explain," continued Paden. Grace noticed he was gesturing behind her.

Us? She thought. She was immediately startled at a deep roar of a voice behind her.

"Let us help you, Grace."

It was him. The dirty, heavyset man from the start of the voyage. The one who threatened Paden on deck. For some reason, Paden had serious issues with him. And now, Grace had been unknowingly pulled into his world of trouble.

Foreword view of the Bridge, Boat Deck, Upper Promenade Deck, and Lower Promenade Deck

Chapter 6

Grace's mouth struggled for words to say, like someone who had experienced a stroke. Her lips tried moving, but nothing came out.

"Grace, you don't know me," spoke the large man, as he stepped towards her.

She reached out her hand to accept his. Her hand dwarfed inside his rough-skinned hand. It felt as though she were rubbing her hand along raw tree bark.

"I'm Ivan Crall. These are my engines," he said, gesturing around and above him, towards the towering steel structures, as they pulsed and pounded with activity. "Each of these engines is connected to one of the ship's propellers out there. That's right," he responded to Grace's shocked reaction. "You are in very deep water, now."

The man stared at Grace for several seconds, as though he warranted some kind of response. As though, she was supposed to be impressed, or have heard of him. His glazed brown eyes burned through his dark, out-of-control eyebrows. *What does he want me to say?* she thought. "Have you brought me here for a reason?" she finally asked.

He didn't answer. Glancing back at Paden, then back at her, he spoke again. "Didn't you tell her the whole story?" he said with a scowl, but only looking at Grace, not Paden. Grace feared that Paden might be in trouble for not following the man's instructions somehow.

"I told her, but she wouldn't really believe me…she needed to see. We can explain it now. Then, she'll believe."

Grace looked at the two of them. The eager, jovial Paden that she had met earlier, seemed to have been replaced by a trance-like figure. He stared at Grace with slow, deliberate wide-eyes, as though he was a zombie.

"Paden, do you need me anymore?"

"Uh, just give us a minute," answered Paden to Eddie, who was standing off at the large doorway. Eddie had his hands in his pockets, and whistled a tune while he listened to the response. Paden had been torn from his shroud of mystique, and seemed sober again.

"Paden, I want to leave," said Grace, giving a quick glance at Crall, then back at Paden.

"Leave, you shall, Ms. Hathaway, but with some information and intent," spoke Crall, approaching Grace and Paden. "You see, I have uncovered a plot by some aboard this ship to steal your father's silver, right out from under him. Do you want that to happen?"

"No, of course not," she answered. "But, who would be able to do that? How do you know—"

"Listen very carefully. The question concerning you right now isn't who, or how, or even why. The situation is that very soon, unless you do something about it, it will happen, and your father won't be enjoying his stay in First Class, to say the least."

Grace answered the man, in more direct and bold speech. "What do you care of my father? Why should I believe your concern for him?"

"My concern isn't for your father, Ms. Hathaway. That should be yours. My concern is that I've been a part of this ship since the first bolt of steel was pounded into her sturdy hull back at Fairfield shipping yard, in Scotland. I told you—these engines are mine. This ship is mine. I've gained quite the reputation and pride for looking after her. I'll not let some greedy lot, in search of a fast fortune, tarnish her name with a scandal of thievery."

Grace looked to Paden for a sign from his face that the man was being truthful. It was unclear. "Paden, I—"

"Listen, Grace, you must believe us. What you need to do is to help us…" he said looking upward, as though searching for the right word, "acquire the silver. We must take it and hide it."

Grace was about to respond, but was cut off.

"Only until then, can we be assured of its safety."

"So, you say someone will steal the silver, and I am to help you steal it first. How can I be assured that it isn't you who are stealing the silver?"

Paden turned aside to Crall. Crall responded to Paden. "I told you this wouldn't work. We're wasting our time."

Paden continued. "You just 'ave to trust us. I mean, do you really think we would try to steal the silver, and tell you about it first?"

"It's possible," she said. "And besides, why not let my father in on the plot? Or the ships' officers?"

"Grace, we don't know who to trust, really. We could be helpin' out the thieves, if we let on that we know." Paden's wandering eyes appeared to be thinking of another angle to pitch at her. "All right, then. I'll even show you where we plan to hide it." He grabbed her by the arm, led her around the engine, along a passageway, then stopped at a part of the ship's hull. Grace saw Paden reach along the metal bulkhead, as though he were looking for something. She noticed a small crack. Then, a bigger one, as

Paden shimmied open a portion of the hull that started near his waist, and continued up to his head. It was roughly square in shape, and inside there was a crawlspace of some kind.

"What is this?" she asked.

"This conduit leads to a service area. It rarely gets opened. In fact, most people don't even know it's 'ere. The cap'n probably wouldn't even notice it. This is where we can hide your father's silver, once we bag it in those mail sacks."

Grace glanced at the open tube, at Paden, then back at Crall, whose melon of a head could be seen hanging around the end of the engines. She didn't know what to believe. It seemed so preposterous. But, what if it were true? She wouldn't want anything to happen to her father, or his reputation. She decided that she didn't have enough answers. She had been reading her mystery book on the train, earlier, but didn't feel any more qualified to solve this mystery. She could easily see how Crall might be a villain, trying to deceive her. But, Paden, too. And what about Eddie, the pastry guy? He was probably still standing in the doorway, hands in his pockets, with pastry flour on his nose and a jovial melody on his lips. How could he intend her any harm? He would be the least likely suspect in this caper...if it were a caper. The most likely suspect...Crall, and maybe even Paden, now.

"Well, Grace?" spoke Paden, looking for assurance of assistance.

"What is it you plan to do? What was with the grand tour you gave me?" she asked, hoping for evidence, either way, to lead her to the truth.

"The reason I took you 'round the ship, like I did, was to show you that we have it all planned. It is a foolproof plan. While guarding outside the steward's office where the silver is locked away, the officers will become very sleepy. That is, with the assistance of a drink, laced with the medicine I got from the good doctor."

Grace gasped. "I knew you were faking that injury."

"Then the officers will be temporarily replaced with two newly promoted ones, a.k.a., myself and Fast Eddie. We'll use the galley cart that you rode in to house the silver, escort it to the lift, and bring it down here to hide. If the cap'n gets any wind of the action, there just might be an 'accidental' fire on the bridge to keep him and the other crew busy…thank you, Murph'. All in all, a brilliant plan, I think," he said with assurance.

"Do you really think it will work?" asked Grace, with scepticism.

"It better work," spoke Crall's hoarse tone on the back of her neck, causing her to jump.

She relaxed after the initial shock of his proximity, and surmised that Paden must have come up with the plan. *Crall will not be too happy, if it fails*, she thought. "Paden, it seems you have worked everything out…but, haven't you forgotten one very important detail?"

"What's that?" he asked.

"How are you going to get the silver out of the safe? Only my father knows the combination. He won't willingly give that information up."

"You're right, Grace," continued Paden. "That's where you come in. We need you to get your father to open the safe again, so that you can watch him as he dials the numbers. Then you can tell us the combination."

"Deceive my own father?"

"It will benefit him in the end," responded Paden. "His silver will be saved."

"And what about you, Paden? Aren't you concerned about deceiving your father, too?"

"It will help him in the end, too. He'll be proud of me for helping save the silver. Now, let's get back to your job. We need you to get your father to the safe."

"And how am I supposed to do that, exactly? He's probably in bed by now." She glanced at her watch. Almost 9:10. He would probably retire earlier tonight because of the long journey. "What? Am I supposed to simply say, 'Father, I'm sorry to interrupt your sleep, but I want to have a wee peek at the silver?' You will have to do better than that."

"What is that around your neck, Grace?" asked Paden, pointing to Grace's heart-shaped necklace.

"My mother gave it to me, just before she died. It carries her picture," said Grace hesitantly.

"Then it is dear to you, then?" interjected Crall, once again slithering up to Grace.

"Yes, of course."

"Tell your father," he continued, "that you are concerned for its safety, and you want to see it stowed away somewhere."

"Yes," continued Paden. "He may even suggest the safe himself. In light of his losing his wallet earlier, he may be more receptive to the idea."

Grace stood clutching her necklace. She looked at the two men, both staring at her. She didn't know what to do. She couldn't make any reckless decisions now. She would have to wait. She burst out, "I need time. I need to think. I...want to go above. Maybe then, I'll consider your offer."

Crall remained motionless for a moment, then slid his giant arm down from a bulkhead he had been leaning on and made a hissing sound with his teeth in the direction of Paden.

Paden spoke to Grace. "All right, then. Eddie will take you back up. Go to your room and think. But don't think too long. Ya' might not have that much time. Word is: it's going down tonight."

Grace would have liked to ask more questions, but was more concerned with getting back to her deck, above the waterline. She needed clarity.

"Fast Eddie," spoke Paden as he led Grace back around the giant engine, towards the doorway where they had previously entered. Crall stayed a step behind. "Grace would like to return to the upper decks. Can you take her back? Back through the galley?"

"No problem, Paden," spoke Eddie with a headshake and a wink at Grace. "Follow me, Ms. Hathaway."

Grace was about to follow Eddie out of the large engine room, but made one last turn before leaving. She noticed Paden handing a brown leather wallet to Crall. At first, she wondered if it was her father's wallet. Same colour. But, her father's was returned. She was still close enough to the pair to see that the wallet had an imprint of a crest on it. Some type of circular symbol, with a cross in the middle, and what appeared to be a crown on top.

Paden looked up and saw that Grace was watching him, and she immediately turned again and left with Eddie. Whatever she had just witnessed, it didn't seem right. There was something else going on. Grace barely had time to contemplate the situation before she was forced to skip ahead to keep up with Fast Eddie.

"Sorry to be so hasty, Ms. Hathaway. Some passengers will be looking to point some blame for their tardy cream puffs if I don't hurry back above."

Grace continued through the same way she came, but made certain that she kept up with her leader, as she didn't want to risk becoming lost below the depths. After a few more quick turns, Grace was back at the lift, and ascending with Eddie. She couldn't help but have a soft spot for him. He seemed quite content—free of worry. Grace was shaking with confusion, fear, weariness. Paden and Crall appeared uptight, and anxious. Eddie was none of these. *Perhaps he is ignorant of the events taking place. He could be just a pawn in the game Paden and Crall are playing.*

The lift reached its intended destination and halted with a slight bounce. Both Eddie and Grace stared at each other, as though each was waiting for something to happen. Grace was waiting for Eddie to open the door so she could manoeuvre her way around the dessert cart that remained in the lift from their descent into the depths. Eddie's intentions for waiting became clear when he head-nodded Grace's stare to the cart that separated them at the waistline.

"What?" Grace said, "back in there? You can forget it! I've had enough playing along." When she uttered these words, she realized that her 'playing along' would just be about to start, if she followed Paden's plan.

"All right, then, Ms. Hathaway. Let me check." He slid open the lift door a crack and ushered his right eye up to the opening. After a few seconds, he turned back and nodded to Grace. "Things have slowed down. Only Josef is in the galley. When you get out, make a quick left and follow the checked floor to the exit. I'll distract him."

The door made a slight knocking, but Grace was able to get out without Josef turning around from the sink where he was washing his hands. Grace carefully trod on the floor so that her boot heels wouldn't 'click' too hard, while she saw Eddie stride up beside the man. "Josef," he began, "you're working too hard this evening…" and then his voice trailed off as Grace somehow arrived back in the passageway where she had entered with Paden and Eddie earlier.

Grace stood in the passageway for a moment and couldn't remember exactly how to get back to her cabin. Rather than sleeping, she now wondered if her father would be standing in the doorway, wondering what became of her. Why she was gone, and with whom, if anyone. She should hurry back upstairs. She stole a look at her watch. 9:20.

Exiting the passageway, Grace realized she was in the Second Class Dining Saloon again, through which she had passed with Paden, following their visit to the doctor. She realized that she was heading in the wrong direction for her room. Although she was heading to the aft section of the ship, she thought she should remain with what was familiar. She continued on through the Dining Saloon, where lingering dinner guests finished their tea and coffee.

Entering the Second Class Social Hall, she immediately noticed several of the Salvationists who were entertaining themselves and others in song. One uniformed man played a lively tune on the piano. In any other situation, Grace would have liked to stay and listen. Possibly, join along. Show what she could do. Instead, she was forced to allow the chords to sail off as she exited onto the deck.

She found a staircase and made her way up on Lower Promenade Deck. She was happy to be outside in the open air again, having been deep in the bowels of the ship without any sense of familiarity. As she strolled along the port side, the breeze lifting her hair once again, she noticed dim lights passing off in the distance. It was another ship.

Once again, Grace could hear music playing, and noticed several other Salvationists singing as they strolled along the deck, like carollers might do at Christmas time. "Our sins are washed away," Grace heard sung, until she was distracted by one of the lot.

An older gentleman in the group turned to another. "My wallet," he exclaimed. "It's missing."

Grace was about to overtake the singers, when she slowed to listen, acting as though she were looking out at the moon.

"Something has happened to my wallet."

A few of the others stopped singing and one man asked, "When did you last see it?" as he and the man looked around on the deck floor.

"What does it look like?" asked another.

An unusual question, thought Grace. *It looks like a wallet. It's not like the deck floor is going to be scouring with them. Find one, and it's a safe bet that it is his.*

"My wife gave it to me, before we left. It has our crest on it."

Upon hearing this, Grace realized her biggest fears were being realized. Paden had stolen this man's wallet. Stolen his wallet, and given it to Crall. There was a thief ring aboard the ship, after all. Paden was part of it. The conspiracy to steal the silver. It had to be a fairy tale. "Save the silver," she muttered, "save it for you, you mean, Paden." She was furious. Furious with Paden, but more furious with herself, allowing herself to be taken in.

She decided she had seen enough and resolved to walk past the group. As she did, the glow of the ship's lights cast recognition upon the victim's face. Grace stopped for a moment in surprise, but continued on. It was him—the older man from the send-off at the port. Paden had stolen the wallet of the Salvationist who had somehow offended him with his words. *A lowly thing to do,* she thought. *Stealing from this man! He seemed kind, and well meaning.*

Grace pulled into a doorway, determined to get to her room before her father called a ship-wide search, and to go to bed. She was tired of games. Turning to go up the hallway to her room, she bumped into someone. "Sorry," was her immediate reaction. "I...Eddie?"

"Sorry, Ms. Hath—"

"But, how did you get here so—"

"My name, remember?"

"Fast Eddie," they both said simultaneously.

"I have to keep moving," he told her. "Mr. Steele is out. Making sure his crew are doing their jobs. I just spoke with him before you came. He was looking for Paden."

"Look, Eddie. You can tell Paden I won't have any part of his treachery. He's a thief and a liar…and who knows what else."

She marched up the hall away from Eddie, towards her room, without glancing back. When she approached her room, she could hear music playing again. It was coming from the Music Room. *This ship never sleeps*, she thought. Before reaching the Music Room, she made a hard right to her room door. Grace crafted the handle open so as not to disturb her father, in the event that he was already sleeping. *What would he say about her disappearance?* she wondered. As she stepped into the darkness, the only source of light was the moonlight shining through the window. She stood motionless for a moment to assess the situation. No breathing could be heard. *Is he here?* As she listened for other sounds, her eyes had assimilated the darkness and she discovered that her father's bedclothes lay flat. *He is not here.*

Grace engaged the electric light and stood for a moment with her hands on her hips. "Where are you, father?" she said in frustration. In her mind, she knew. He was most certainly in the Music Room with Harriet and other elite travellers, sipping champagne whilst listening to ship's musicians on the piano and other instruments. Once again, she was alone. The only companionship she would endure since coming aboard the ship was a young thief.

She sat on her father's lower bed. Looking across the room, she noticed her book lying atop her baggage in the middle of the floor. She snatched it and began reading again to distract herself from the evening's events before sleeping.

"The Wilkshire Mansion murder remains a mystery at this point," spoke investigator Taylor, "but sometimes in order to find out 'who' is responsible, we must ask 'why'. Taylor glanced around the roomful of suspects, each with

their own motive and possible alibi. "Some kill for revenge," he said, making a deliberate glance across to Mr. Shackleby, seated on the sofa and giving a surprised look. "Others," he said with a spin round the room, finally fixing his gaze on Mrs. Sheldrake, "will kill because they are under duress, and feel as though they are out of options. They need salvation, but resort to the most final of methods, rather than seeking assistance from others, or from admitting their own helplessness…"

Grace put her book down. She couldn't help but think about Paden. She was angry with him, for certain. However, she couldn't help but read him into this story. Paden wasn't a murderer—at least, she hoped not. But, his encounter earlier with Crall up on deck, did signal duress. Perhaps, Crall was forcing him into his employment. Paden himself, told Grace that 'everyone needs savin' at some point in their life.' Grace couldn't help but feel that Paden needed saving, and that she was the one who would have to do it. She had failed Andrew. She couldn't make the same mistake twice.

Grace jumped. It was a knock at the door. "Father?" she spoke as she rose to her feet. No one entered the room, or even touched the door handle. She reached towards the door with her hands, wondering if she should open it, but hesitated as she felt something sliding under her left boot. Looking down, she noticed white. It was a white envelope with writing. Her name. She stooped down to retrieve the note and tore it open. She began reading:

Grace,

If you want Paden Thomas to see the light of day ever again, you must get that combination number. His, and your survival will depend on it.

Anon.

That was it. Paden seemed to be in trouble. Either he was seriously facing physical harm if he didn't come up with the silver for Crall, or he was part of a more elaborate lie than Grace had predicted. She could stay in her room and wait things out, but knew she wouldn't be able to sleep without knowing the truth. Clutching the handle, she swung the door open wide and stepped out. She had to find Paden, wherever he was aboard this ship.

Galley on Shelter Deck.

Chapter 7

As Grace rounded the corner of the hall, she could still hear strains of music floating through the frosted pane of the Music Room door. She had better avoid that way entirely or she might run into her father. She wouldn't be able to wander off then, but would be coaxed into her bed. *It could be worse*, she thought. *I might run into—*

"Where have you been?" demanded a shrill voice as Grace turned away from the Music Room.

"Harriet? Oh, dear. You frightened me. What are you—"

"Frightened you? Is that all you care about? You? While you have been gallivanting off, 'who knows where', your father has been left with the burden of finding his daughter."

"You mean, he's not with you, then?" asked Grace.

"He was. That is, until he realized you hadn't returned to your quarters."

The conversation turned from horrible to grotesque at the mention of that word. 'Quarters'. Grace was neither in the military, nor was Harriet her commanding officer. She never would be.

"And where have you been all this time?" demanded Harriet.

"All this time? Exactly, how long has father been searching for me?" inquired Grace, as a measure of her father's concern.

"He departed only moments ago. He left the music lounge to go fetch his spectacles, when he noticed you missing."

Grace had momentarily felt genuine concern coming from her father. That is, until she discovered her father's half-hearted effort. He hadn't noticed her gone until recently. *I suppose I should be grateful that he has left Harriet and is searching for me,* she consoled herself.

"Well, here I am," spoke Grace nonchalantly, throwing her arms in the air. She couldn't think of anything else to say, and didn't feel Harriet merited the effort.

"Is that all you can say? 'Here I am!'" mocked Harriet.

"You are right, Harriet. I need to say more. I need to do more. I should go rescue...search for father. So that he won't be out all night searching for me." Grace knew her father really did need saving...from Harriet. But, for the moment, the excuse to go look for him would suffice for an opportunity to find Paden. She turned her back on her stepmother-to-be.

"Wait! You can't just leave!"

"I have to. For father's sake. I shan't be long," she stated as she heard trailings of Harriet's voice behind her. Grace didn't turn to look back, but could tell Harriet was not following her. Grace felt it best to avoid heavy populated areas, so that she wouldn't run into her father. She needed to find Paden somehow. It wouldn't be easy. This was a big ship, and no doubt, he would have left the lower decks by now. She decided the best means of action would be to ask Fast Eddie. He would be easier to find. In the galley. She would take the same evasive course that she had plotted moments earlier. Out on deck. Down its long outdoor passageway to the back of the ship, and in through the Second Class sections. As she began to pass through the strong double doors leading outside into the night, she heard a commanding voice.

"Ms. Hathaway!"

She made the mistake of turning back. It was Mr. Steele. Should she keep going and act as though she hadn't heard or seen him? This would arouse suspicion, for she had made a definite turn back towards him. She decided she should engage Mr. Steele for a moment.

"Mr. Steele. How are things?"

"Just cheery," he said, although Grace couldn't tell if he was being sarcastic or not. "Have you seen Mr. Thomas? The young Mr. Thomas, that is."

"Should I have?" she replied.

"You were spotted with him earlier. I thought that perhaps you still knew of his whereabouts."

Grace thought that the best course of action was to be evasive, until she could find Paden herself. "He left me sometime ago. Said he had some ship's business to do. Helping some passengers down below, I believe." *Don't get too carried away*, she said to herself, for her extra remarks in defence of Paden.

"Really? And may I ask where you are off to? A young lady shouldn't be out in the dark, late at night."

Grace couldn't decide whether she was flattered by Mr. Steele's gentlemanly remarks, or whether she felt that he was too controlling. He had the natural look and charm of a stage star, but made Grace feel as though he was acting too concerned.

"I'm just getting a bit of fresh evening air. Seeing that this is the first night on the ship. That is all. I'll be retiring shortly."

He hesitated for a moment with a suspicious squint, but then smiled and said, "Very well. Good evening," as he tipped his cap. He held the burdensome door open so that Grace could pass through to the night. "And remember," he added, "if you see Mr. Thomas, please inform me. I shall be about."

"Sure thing, Mr. Steele." Grace shivered as she walked away down the darkened deck. *Why didn't I fetch a shawl when I was in the room?* she scolded herself. A few passengers remained out on deck, but she did not meet with the travelling musicians this time. As she continued towards the Second Class area, she couldn't help but think about Mr. Steele's last words. *'If you see Mr. Thomas, please inform me.' Curious,* she thought. *Why didn't he say, 'If you see Mr. Thomas, please tell him to see me,' or 'Please tell him I am looking for him?' Could it be that he doesn't want Paden to know that he is looking for him? Is he trying to trap Paden? Perhaps, he has become aware of Paden's plan to steal the silver...I have to find Paden, before he gets arrested.*

Grace rushed along Lower Promenade Deck, then made her way down to Shelter Deck, through the Second Class area, into the passageway, then to the door of the galley. She surprised herself how quickly she made it there, now that she was becoming quite accustomed to the ship and her layout.

Peering through the round glass window, she could see the backs of several crewmembers in white. She wanted to invite herself in, but didn't want to cause a disruption that might lead to questions about who she was, or where she was going. Standing in the passageway with indecision, she was relieved to see one of the crewmen turn around. It was Eddie.

"Eddie," she spoke in a loud whisper as she cracked open the door.

He centred his stare at her. "Ms. Hathaway?" He walked to the passageway and joined Grace. "What are you doing? I thought you were off to bed."

"I thought you were two decks up," she returned.

"I was. That's why they call me—"

"I know. Fast Eddie, right? Listen. I must find Paden."

"Paden? I thought you were done with him. You said—"

"I know what I said. But, I want to speak with him."

"He's meeting me down on Upper Deck in a few minutes."

"Isn't that an oxymoron?"

"A what?"

"Never mind. Take me with you."

Grace followed Eddie once again. But this time, they did not use the lift. She was thankful that she wasn't going into the depths of the ship. The thought of being trapped so far below the waterline, even though the chance of water coming in seemed remote, gave her a sinking feeling in her stomach. They moved through the Second Class Dining Room, exited, then descended a set of stairs, taking them from Shelter Deck, down to Upper Deck.

Grace noticed a room at the bottom of the stairs that appeared to be a nursery. It was empty, as most children would probably be in bed at this hour. Eddie led Grace along a corridor on the starboard side that dissected a number of areas of the ship. Passenger cabins. A service room. Ladies lavatory. Other doors simply had numbers posted on them. *These must be restricted to crew*, she thought.

After cutting a straight line towards the bow of the ship, Eddie pointed out an open area. Straight ahead, she could see a fenced area, with a few people standing around it. One of them was Paden. He appeared to be speaking with a young couple, probably in their thirties.

"There he is," said Eddie, as he stopped Grace by taking her arm with his hand.

"What are you doing?" she questioned him.

"There's something I need to tell you about Paden," he said, looking serious for the first time since she had met him.

"What is it?" she asked curiously.

He pointed to the fenced area. She could now tell that it was a sandpit. A playground. There was a young child. A girl. Maybe four or five years of age. Playing joyfully in the sand. She wondered why this child was still awake at this hour. She noticed the child moving towards Paden and the assumed parents were leaning on the fenced rail. Grace turned her head sideways and listened carefully. She was just close enough to make out their conversation over the low hum of the ship's engines.

"We normally don't allow sweets at this late hour, Mr. Thomas," spoke the father to Paden. "But," he said hesitantly, "this is the first night on the ship. A cause for celebration. Little Anna has never been on a ship like this one before. That's why we permitted her to stay up and play. She's too excitable to go to bed just yet."

"She'll probably be up all night," interjected the mother.

"The both of us, on the other hand," added the father, "will most likely die when we hit the pillow."

Grace wondered what the significance of this event was as she noticed Paden offer a tray of sweets to this little girl, covered in sand from her toes to her curls poking out of her hat. She took a pastry and devoured it with a smile to Paden.

"Anna," spoke the mother. "What do you say to the kind crewman?"

"Doo, koo," came the muffled mumble from the stuffed treats.

"I think that was, 'thank you,'" she said, reassuring Paden.

Grace turned to Eddie. "Are these the treats you had in the lift? Is this the errand Paden spoke about?"

"Yes."

"You people tell me that a crime is going to take place on this ship, tonight, and there's time to deliver sweets?" questioned Grace, shaking her head.

"It only took a small bit of time for Paden to come here. No worry. It's something he likes to do. Give gifts to the children. He does it all the time."

"You mean gifts stolen from the galley?" she asked.

"The spirit in it is right, Ms. Hathaway."

"Don't tell me. A modern-day Robin Hood? Please!"

Eddie turned to Grace and threw the same serious face he had given her moments before. "Understand, Ms. Hathaway. Paden is no saint. I'll give you that. But, he has his good side, too. He has had his share of misfortune."

"Like?"

"Well," said Eddie, seeming reluctant, "he once had a sister. She died, just a few years ago. When she was small. Much like that little girl over there. It was on her birthday."

Grace gasped as she looked over at the young child in the sand, making a connection with Paden's little sister. "How did she die?"

"Some kind of illness. I don't know, really. Paden doesn't get into it. The important thing is that he was wounded that day. He had been out on the streets of London, with some of his mates. He was involved in…well…trouble."

"Pick-pocketing?" asked Grace, boldly.

"Precisely. He was in with a bad lot. Anyway, he promised his parents…his sister, that he would be back in time for her birthday celebration. He ran out of time. He arrived home late in the evening. Just after the visiting doctor pronounced her dead. He never saw her again. I suppose, his kindness to children on this ship are his way of attempting to make up for it."

"He's giving them the gifts that he didn't give his sister. Some sort of redemption."

"You could say that," said Eddie.

"How do you ever make up for something like that?" asked Grace.

"Maybe ya' can't," came a voice.

Grace looked to the side. It was Paden. She and Eddie both hadn't noticed him approach from the sandpit.

"You can only keep on tryin'," he continued.

"Paden. I didn't hear you approach," said Grace apologetically.

"T'was obvious," he said plainly.

Grace was not certain how to proceed with the conversation. She came down to see him. To yell at him. To get mad at him. To warn him. She wasn't sure which. Now, she was even more confused. Should she feel sorry for him, now that she has witnessed his vulnerable side?

"I'll see you shortly," said Eddie to Paden. He made a hasty turn, and exited.

Grace wondered if he was leaving before Paden could chastise him for leaking secrets of his personal life.

"Later, Eddie," nodded Paden.

"Listen, Paden," spoke Grace. "I'm sorry to hear about your sister."

"That's none of your business," he said sharply. "The only thing you should be worryin' yourself o'er is getting that combination. We have to move quickly."

"That's why I came searching for you."

"There a problem?"

"Of course there's a problem, Paden. You come to me, wanting me to trust you. Seeming sincere. Then you lie to me."

"Lie to you? What do you mean?" he asked, with the same sense of sincerity on his face as before.

"This whole plot to steal the silver. Is there really a plot? Or is it simply your plot to steal the silver?"

"That's quite the accusation, Grace."

Grace was feeling as though the conversation was going

nowhere. She would have to expedite matters. "You are a thief! You stole that man's wallet!"

"What man are—"

"You know. The Salvationist on deck. As we were leaving port. I saw you giving it to Crall. The fact that you are denying it now, only supports your guilt further. You are a fraud. For all I know, you stole Father's wallet, too. And, I believe it is you who are going to steal the silver, and keep it for yourself."

"Grace, we don't 'ave time for this. We must—"

"We have to make time for it, Paden. Making time for things seems to be your weakness. Isn't that right, Paden?" Grace spoke these words in anger. She was hinting, in no subtle way, that he had failed his sister. She wondered if she had sunk too low in her remarks.

"Look, Grace. I don't need you, or anyone else telling—" Paden looked around. He seemed to be conscious of the few passengers that were still lingering near the playground, particularly, the young family that he had been speaking with.

"That's just it, Paden. You do need me. You need me to get that combination number. You need me, or there will be nothing in it for you!"

Paden took Grace by the arm and led her back into the passageway. He spoke in a loud whisper as they stopped at the entrance of the long hallway. "In it for me? In it for me?" he repeated. "You don't know what's in it for me. Sure, I stole the old man's wallet. It's Crall who wants it. He has some of us steal so that he can pay his people. It keeps 'em loyal. That way he can use them, whenever he wants. And your father's wallet. Yes, I stole that too. But, only for information. I had to be certain I had the right family. I had to make sure that he was Mr. Hathaway, and that perhaps, he had written the combination number down in his

112

wallet. Sounds desperate, I know. But, these are desperate times. I had to use whatever advantages I could get."

"And your befriending of me? Were you using me for the sake of gaining an advantage too?"

"Yes," he answered coldly. "But, I had to. Crall wants that silver, and will stop at nothing to get it."

"Then, was it him who sent me that note?" asked Grace.

"Note? What note?" answered Paden.

He seemed genuine in his questioning, but Grace had fallen for that look before. Grace paused for a moment to think. She and Paden had been more forthcoming in this conversation than any before. "Why are you telling me all this now? Surely, you don't think I'm going to help you get rich now?"

"That's just it, Grace. I'm hoping that by telling you everything, you will help me. You see, I'm not doing this to get rich."

Grace pulled her head back slightly in doubt.

"I'm doing this to get my family back together."

"Your family?"

"Yes. My father and I are on this ship because we can't afford to live at home. I told you, my mother works for the rich people of London. My father feels he has to work at sea to support her. When my sister died, my father took it hard, as did my mother and I. She died because he didn't 'ave enough money to get her to a proper hospital. Even if he did, she would have needed medicine. That alone would have been costly. The day of her funeral, he vowed never to return home 'til he had enough money to look after his family."

"Does he blame you for your sister's death?"

"Maybe not for her death. But, for not being there with her, before she died. I thought there was time. I never dreamt of running out of time. The only words Father, always the seaman,

113

spoke to me the day of her funeral were: 'Time is an unstoppable wave that rolls over us all.' If only I had realized that earlier." Paden paused in thought for a moment, then continued. "That night, I was out, milling around Booth Park with me mates. Up to no good," said Paden, juggling a glistening, round silver object out from his right trouser pocket. "I looked at my newly acquired timepiece here and realized it was late. I immediately headed home, only to see the look of death on peoples' faces as I cracked open the house door."

"Paden. You can't blame yourself," said Grace. *But, then again, he could.*

"You know," he continued, "I went back to the park everyday for the next week. Timed the walk from the park to my house, again and again. You know what it was?"

Grace shrugged her shoulders.

"Fourteen minutes. Fourteen minutes was all that kept me from seeing my sister alive, one last time. If only I had left fourteen minutes earlier. But, my stolen timepiece could not 'elp me steal time back. Those moments would never be counted again." Paden straightened up, and continued. "That is why my father is always checkin' up on me, about 'ow I spend the time. Am I on time for duty? Will I have time to complete my duties? Can I be counted on as consistently as time itself?"

"Sounds like a noble gesture," suggested Grace.

"Perhaps. But, I much more respect your father's sense of time."

"How's that?" asked Grace squinting.

"You said earlier that he was a man of business. Swift action. That's what I respect. Takin' charge. 'Stead of waitin' for time to catch up and cooperate."

Grace didn't give his words much thought. Her father seemed

rather selective in the area of time. She switched the conversation back on Paden. "Why are you here with your father?"

"I'm here because…well, because he couldn't trust me. I was gettin' into some trouble back home, and my parents thought it would be best if I be under the watchful eye of my father. That's why he is always on me. Doesn't trust me. Doesn't respect me. You've seen 'ow he is with me. Can't even bring himself to salutin' me, like a real crew member."

"It seems to me that you're always stealing away from your duties," suggested Grace. "Plotting with Crall down below. Now, delivering goodies to children in Third Class, on Upper Deck. Doesn't he have a right to be suspicious?"

"I'm not exactly down 'ere for nothin'. See that lever over there," he said, head motioning a few feet behind her. "That there is me main responsibility. I also came to check on it. Make sure it was in workin' order."

Grace looked to see a metal bar poking up from the floor, and finishing about waist high. "What is it?"

"It's a gear. It operates a watertight door, directly below on Main Deck. In the case of a disaster, and mostly just routine drills, I 'ave to make sure that the crank key gets put on properly. Then, I turn the gear all the way to shut the door below. Takes 'bout a minute, at best."

Grace tried to encourage Paden. "That seems like a noble task. Your father must have confidence in you to entrust you with that job."

"Not really. It's more of a sentencing, than a responsibility. Like a judge would give a criminal. Father caught me slouching off, about a week ago. As a punishment, he assigned me to additional duties, above my regular shift. Every morning at 10, we 'ave a drill. I'm down 'ere crankin' away, sweatin' through my clothes, and whose head do I see peerin' at me from down the hall?"

"Your father?"

"You knows it. You see, he doesn't trust me enough to believe that I would make it 'ere alone. Not only is it a prison sentence, 'aving to come down 'ere all the time, it shows he doesn't 'ave the faith in me."

"Well, maybe not yet, anyway. But, he will sometime, I'm sure."

Paden shrugged his shoulders. "Anyways. Enough of that."

Grace returned to the issue at hand. "What do you hope to achieve with all this silver?"

"I don't want all the silver. I just want enough to give our family the means to get back together in London. Crall can have the rest. That's the deal. I help him, and I get my cut. If I don't, then I might get a different type of cut, if ya' knows what I mean. Even if I wanted to back out now, Crall would be after me. He has people working for him all over this ship. I don't even know who they all are."

Grace shook her head. "Paden, you have gotten yourself into quite the mess. And me too, I'm afraid." She thought for a moment. "Why don't you tell your father about Crall? You could easily earn his respect if you helped him save the silver. He would stop doubting you then."

"I don't think even that would change his mind. All I want is to see that my family's future is secure."

Paden's words caused Grace to think of something she had read. She thought out loud.

"Uncertainty and expectation are the joys of life. Security is an insipid thing."

"What?" questioned Paden.

"It's something I read once. A man named William Congreve penned it," explained Grace.

"Let me guess. Another book you have read?"

"His point was that if you always see the road ahead of you, then it wouldn't be worth taking the journey."

"Do you always live by what you read in books?" asked Paden.

"Usually," she replied, honestly. "Perhaps you should take up reading. It might help you make wiser decisions."

"Are you saying you won't help me?"

"It's not a good idea."

"Why?" he insisted. "Because you read it in a book? Well, let me tell you something: life isn't a book!" Paden's voice trembled and his face shot red. "Life is not scripted. You have to show some hint of independence and initiative at a certain point, Grace."

"Initiative? You don't know me enough, Paden. I have initiative. I do things on my own."

"Then why are you aboard this ship? I'm right sure it wasn't your idea. But, because you didn't show enough independence of your own, you 'ave followed your father's scripting."

Grace folded her arms in disgust, about to reply, but was cut off.

"You have to start writing your own book, Grace, where each new page is penned by Grace Hathaway, and not by someone else."

Grace knew he was reflecting back on what she had told him about Harriet and her father. Her lower lip quivered as she attempted a defence. "Your comparison is inaccurate!"

"Is it, Grace?" he continued. "You are truly 'fraid of a little…what did you call it… 'improvisation'?

"And so, what? You are saying I should please you now, too? Wouldn't I be giving in to YOUR script, not my own?"

"But, don't you see, Grace? This can help you too."

"Help me?"

"Yes. You, yourself, told me that you are being forced into

movin' to England with your father and his new bride-to-be. And when I asked you what would 'appen if your father's mine's silver went missing, you said he would end up back home. Back home with a lot of questions to answer, but nonetheless, back home. Isn't that what you want, Grace? To go back home? I get what I want. Crall gets what he wants. And you get what you want. It's a sweet deal all 'round."

Grace had previously settled nicely into being angry with Paden. She had the reason. She had the evidence. She had the nerve. Now, however, she had doubts. She had learned more about him in the past few minutes, speaking with him, than she had since meeting him earlier today. She had fallen prey to his plan, as he used her for various purposes. But, she wasn't certain that they were completely selfish purposes. She identified with his loss of a loved one. She empathized with his desire for a family once again. She lived his desire to return to a native land called home. It might not be the right thing to do, but it seemed to be the only thing to do. Trust Paden. She had just the right amount of anger against her father to do it.

Part of her wondered if someone else was speaking as she said, "Very well, Paden. I will help you steal the silver." She had been here before. She had agreed to help him earlier, but had regretted it. Was she making the same mistake twice?

"Thank you, Grace," said Paden, with an apparent sound of relief and sincerity in his voice.

"Don't thank me yet," she said. "There still remains my father to convince. I have to somehow convince him to open the safe, and I don't think he'll be as trusting as I have been."

Paden broke his eye contact with Grace to look at his watch. "Blimy! It's 9:45. They'll be closin' down the ship's office at 10. If you're going to get to your father, it'll have to be before then. Otherwise, we're done for." He started walking down the hall, past cabins and other doors. They continued their conversation on the move.

"Very well," Grace replied. "Where can I find you once I get the combination?"

"I'll come up with you, then you can find me out on deck. I 'ave to close the portholes. One of my jobs. I just 'ave to be sure to avoid Steele."

Grace and Paden made their way up to Upper Promenade Deck quickly enough. Before Grace knew it, she was approaching her room, and Paden was seen ditching her for the large wooden deck doors.

Grace wasn't certain if her father had made it back, or if he was still in the Music Room. She stopped just shy of the Music Room door. It seemed to have become quieter now and she wondered if passengers were retiring for the night. She decided to head for her room first.

Lifting the handle on the door, Grace entered a lit room.

"Grace? I've been looking for you," spoke her father with a straight look. No smile, but no sense of sternness, either. It was as though he was reserving judgment upon a fair hearing.

"Yes, I know," mumbled Grace. "I just needed some air."

"Well, Grace, it would be prudent for you to be in bed. It has been a long day for all of us. And I'm a little worried about you wandering the ship with this young Mr. Thomas. We don't know very much about him. Mr. Steele spoke with me this evening. Seems he has some concerns for the boy."

Grace was confused by her father's concern. It was her father who had encouraged their companionship at dinner. "Yes, Father," spoke Grace obediently.

"That's fine, Grace," he said. "I shall go and say 'good evening' to Harriet, whilst you get ready for bed."

"Wait Father," she urged. This would be her only chance to

get to the safe. Before he left. "I was wondering if we could put this in the safe." Pulling her necklace out of the top of her dress, her father seemed to be paralysed. *Did he forget about the necklace?* she wondered. *Was it now, an inconvenient reminder?*

He broke from his trance. "We can put it in the safe, certainly, if that is what you wish. I'll make arrangements for it, first thing in the morn—"

"There isn't time!" she burst loudly and quickly. She realized she better not seem too anxious, or it would lead to questions. She corrected her speech. "There might not be time for the crew during their busy schedules tomorrow. Why don't we take care of it now while they are not preoccupied?"

Her father seemed to be reading her face. "Is there something the matter, Grace? Something you aren't telling me?"

Passengers strolled the lengthy Promenade Decks

Chapter 8

Grace tried to put on her best 'pity face'. She felt that it would almost be natural at this point.

"Very well," her father said. "I'll see if the purser's office is still open."

"I would like to come, too. Just to keep you company," she added.

"But, the hour is late, Grace."

"I know, but," Grace said as she stammered for a good excuse, "I don't want to be alone." The words slipped from her lips. She was trying to create a lie, but inadvertently spoke how she truly felt. Her father had abandoned her, replaced her mother, caused her to feel as though she had no one on this earth to notice her. Boarding this ship had not made a difference. He remained loyal to Harriet. While Paden was troubled and had ulterior motives, at least he noticed Grace. Paid attention to her. Listened to her.

"Come quickly, then, my dear," said her father.

He led Grace towards the Music Room. She entered the room and observed only a few remaining passengers being amused by the quiet tinkling of keys on the piano. As they moved through the room, passed Harriet's room, and sailed towards the grand staircase, Grace felt remorse for deceiving her father. She knew the theft of the silver would have serious repercussions on his career. On his plans for a new life. On everything. Yet, she continued to move her feet liturgically, now descending the staircase towards the purser's office.

"My good gentlemen," spoke her father to the two guards seated outside the door of the office. The two men straightened up from a slouched position, as though they had been awakened. "Could I please get into the safe, one last time for the evening?"

"Uh, well…" stuttered one officer with a long, dark moustache.

"I believe," interjected the other, "that Mr. Thomas wishes the purser's office closed now, sir."

Grace's father looked at her, as she gave an obvious desperate look on her face, revealing her urgency. She knew he wouldn't settle for the guard's response. Her father was a man of expediency and quickly sprung into action here. He turned back to the officers. "Certainly, gentlemen, there is some type of an agreement we could work out."

"Sorry, sir," spoke the first officer, who now seemed cured of his stuttering. "Mr. Thomas has given us strict orders, not to let anyone—"

"Is there a problem here?" spoke a voice behind Grace.

She turned around. An officer in uniform, completed with cap and trim. It was Mr. Thomas, Paden's father. He looked directly at Grace for a response, and she wished he would look at one of the others instead.

Finally, her father spoke. "Mr. Thomas. Is it possible that I acquire access to the purser's office to place an item in the safe?"

"An item?"

"Yes, sir. My daughter has an heirloom she is concerned

about," responded her father, lifting Grace's necklace off her neck by its chain.

"We told him you wanted the room locked down, sir," spoke the officer with the long moustache.

Mr. Thomas looked at Grace, then her father. He glanced back at the officers who were standing at attention, apparently trying to impress their superior—an obvious distinction from moments ago when they were stooped over in their comfortable chairs.

"Well, I suppose the hour is not quite ten," he said, pulling out his pocket watch. "Gentlemen, allow Mr. Hathaway access to the safe."

"Thank you, sir," spoke Grace's father. "We'll only be a moment."

One officer turned a key and opened the door. Mr. Thomas turned to walk past Grace and her father. "Good evening," he spoke with a nod as he walked past, and away from them.

"Good evening, sir," spoke her father.

Grace was about to step into the office door, when she heard Mr. Thomas call back to her. "And, Grace. You haven't seen young Mr. Thomas have you? Lately?"

Grace froze, then turned. "Young Mr. Thomas?" she repeated. She hated when people lied and tried to cover up by buying time through repeating the question. It was so obvious, yet it was all she had. "Oh, you mean, Paden. Yes, of course. I mean, no. No, I have not seen him."

"Very well," he returned, spinning around to leave.

Entering the office, she thought for certain that the plan was foiled. Certainly, Mr. Thomas could see through her deception. Yet, he pressed the matter no further. Her father, also seemed to be convinced of her sincerity rather easily.

"The necklace, Grace," spoke her father as he approached the dial of the safe.

Grace bolted several steps across the room to get near her father, whose back was turned from her to the safe. He wasted no time getting to it. She stood beside him as she reached behind her neck to unlatch her chain. She watched her father's hands closely as his fingers spun the round knob of the safe door. Its numbers moved fast. He slowed to focus on specific numbers. *66. 66 right.* She tried to make it appear as though she were struggling to get the chain unhooked, and tilted her head to the floor, as though she weren't watching the safe. Her father couldn't see her eyes being strained upwards and back at his hands. *7. 7 left. Now, back to the right…18. That's it. 66, 7, 18. Right, left, then right.*

He turned the handle, and the safe door opened. Grace was astonished as she looked at the silver bars, sparkling from the reflection of the electric light above, shining down on the opening of the large treasure box.

"Ready, dear?"

Grace had almost forgotten about the necklace. "Yes…here it is," she said, handing him her necklace.

"We mustn't indulge them further. Let's go, Grace," he said as he slammed the heavy metal door, spun the knob, and turned to the door.

Grace studied the numbers in her head during the entire trip upstairs to her cabin, for fear of forgetting. She did not have time to think of the moral implications of her schemes—more accurately, Paden's schemes. All she could think of was her homeland, and how there had to be some perfect reason for her going against her father's will.

They quickly arrived back at their room, where her father opened the door, led her in, and spoke. "Now, Grace. It has been an exhausting day. Please get some rest. I shall go for a few moments to allow you to change into your nightclothes. I believe Harriet wishes to have one last stroll on the deck before turning in. She says the open air helps her sleep better. In any event, I will be back very soon."

"All right, Father," Grace calmly replied.

Her father had no sooner closed the door behind him, when Grace thought, *I have to get that number to Paden.* Time would be of the essence. Her father would return in mere moments. Hurriedly, she took the door handle, poked her head out the door, then left the room. Observing that no one was in sight, particularly her father, she tiptoed across the hall.

Where is Paden? she wondered. *He said he would be on deck closing portholes.* A problem presented itself. Meeting Paden on deck, whilst her father and Harriet were due for a stroll on deck, would be hazardous. She would have to hope that it would be dark enough that if there was a meeting of the two parties, her father would be none the wiser, and would think nothing of it.

She walked briskly down the hall, turned left, then moved outside the heavy door leading onto deck. She started in the aft direction of the ship, for fear of running into her father and Harriet towards the bow. Moving quickly, yet with hesitance, she approached shadows on deck. If she ran into her father, she would have to come up with another lie. Her father was a clever man. It was unlikely he would keep falling for her scripted stretching of the truth. *A couple strolling. Not Paden. A pipe smoker leaning on the rail. Not him. A woman leaning on the rail. Definitely not him.*

She thought she could call out his name. "Paden!" she said in her loudest whisper. Bodies were too far down the deck to know who was calling. "Paden!" she said again. "Ouch!" she yelled as she tripped over a solid object. She felt to the ground and looked closer. It was a deck chair. As she arose, she began to call out again. "Pa—"

"Are you daft?" murmured a voice on her left shoulder, as a

hand came from the right and grabbed her mouth shut. "You're going to wake up all the Third Class passengers with that voice, and they're several decks below."

Grace realized by now that it was Paden's voice. Relieved, yet annoyed, she spoke. "Paden. I have to get back, or father will suspect."

"Do you have the combination numbers?" he asked anxiously.

"I do. It is 66 right, 7 left, and 18 right."

"Well done, Grace. You did it."

"Yes, but I'm not sure what I have done. I may have made the biggest error of my life."

"Relax, Grace. Everything will be fine. You're taking this too seriously."

Grace was shaking. The breeze on deck had subsided slightly, but she was trembling like a sapling in a summer storm. *Of course I'm taking this seriously,* she thought. She was appalled at how confident Paden seemed.

Once again, she thought of her last words with Andrew, as he coaxed her into swimming. He made Grace feel like a silly worrywart for questioning his judgement.

"Relax Grace," he said. "You're too serious all the time." She remembered that Andrew behaved stupidly. He behaved…just like Paden was behaving now.

"I have to go," she said, breaking away from Paden and running up deck in the darkness. She tried to avoid the scattered lighting that was penetrating cabin window curtains for fear of colliding with her father and Harriet.

After passing several shadowed figures, she reached her point of entrance. Entering the hallway that would lead back to her room, she was about to walk to her room when she heard voices. An older couple was walking down her hall towards her. She stole a glance at them but turned her back to avoid eye contact, just in case. She thought she recognized them as a couple from the dinner table, earlier. The woman had sat beside Grace and seemed pre-occupied with speaking about the Titanic. Grace felt she better not catch their attention, as they might be inquisitive about why she was out by herself at this hour.

"And did you hear that adorable little girl, earlier?" spoke the woman to her husband.

Grace allowed the couple to pass as she stood by the door to the deck, her back facing outward. She pretended to be studying her watch.

"The girl," continued the woman, "was so horrified of sailing at sea, that she said, 'Momma, I don't want to sleep by the window.' When the young child's mother asked 'why not, Gracie?' the child said, 'because that's where the water will come in.' Isn't that precious?" exclaimed the woman with a ghastly laugh, one followed up with an equally horrific cough of a chuckle by her husband.

When the couple moved outside, Grace turned and continued en route to her cabin. She passed the five or so cabins, then turned right along the short corridor that led to her room. She entered the room and discovered she had beaten her father back. Quickly, she undressed and changed into her nightclothes. She crawled into bed and decided to turn the light out, even though he was expected shortly. He would enter soon, and would think that she had gone nowhere, but had fallen asleep.

As she lay in bed, she couldn't help but be overtaken by the soft sheets and warm blankets. She had been up early that morning, travelled by train and boat, and had negotiated the stairs and decks of the ship a little too much for her liking. All she wanted to do was sleep. *Somehow*, she thought, *things would be better in the morning.* She was certain that even now, as she lay in bed, operations were being undertaken to take the silver. She should be there, but didn't have the strength. *Things will turn out right. They have to,* she assured herself.

Something about darkness and a comfortable position causes the brain to replay earlier conversations of the day, even if only in fragments. Only moments ago, Grace heard that annoying woman speaking of a young child, somewhere on this ship, who is frightened about the ship sinking. *The woman had the nerve to dismiss the child's fears with a laugh. Children's fears are real, and should not be dismissed,* thought Grace in anger. *Even older children,* she thought, thinking of her own fears of abandonment. *The child feels she needs saving, and people simply ignore it.*

Grace's thoughts wandered to her father. She was somewhat surprised at how naïve he was earlier, believing her story about the necklace and the safe. He was too trusting. Of her, and of Harriet. *Even he needs saving…saving from a miserable life with horrible Harriet. Only, he doesn't know it. And Paden. That cocky laugh. 'Relax Grace. You're too serious.' He's gotten himself in a heap of trouble. He's over his head and doesn't know it.* Again she couldn't help but compare Paden to Andrew. *He's just like him,* she thought. *And look at what happened to Andrew.*

She sat up with a gasp. *Look what did happen to Andrew. He died. He died because of me. He died because I failed to save him. He didn't know he needed saving, and I allowed it. I should have been more assertive. I should have saved him from himself. If I had, he would have still been with us. Only, I did what I always do. Obeyed. Paden was right. I am following someone else's script. Afraid to pen my own. If I don't now, then it will be too late for Paden. I have to…*she waited for the right word…*improvise.*

The crack of a door. The dim glow of light. Then darkness. Her father had entered the room. Grace lay motionless to give the impression she was sleeping. She wanted her father to get to sleep himself so that she could escape the room once more. It was more deception. But, it was necessary to save Paden. Her father jostled around the room. Grace could tell that he was attempting to open and close his baggage slowly and quietly, but was unable to stifle the buckles from their inherent 'tinkling'. After several minutes of the same, interjected by the frequent grunt of a throat attempting to clear itself, Grace heard her father climb the ladder to the top bunk. He slid several times in his sheets. Then became silent. Light breathing slipped into heavy breathing. Heavy breathing bore nasal snorts. She thought that she should allow him a few more minutes of uninterrupted silence, just in case. Then, she would make her move for her robe that she wore over her nightclothes, the one her mother had bought for her during one of her many visits to Toronto. Then, slip her boots on, and negotiate a quiet opening of the door. *Just a few more minutes*, she thought. *I'm so weary. How can I move? It would take...*

What? Grace thought. *What's happening? Where...?* It took her a moment to figure out where she was. *In the cabin...aboard the Empress.* She had fallen asleep. She only wanted to lie still for a few moments, but a few moments in time might now cost dearly. She had no idea what time it was. Only that it was still dark. Still night time. The hum of the engines seemed different now. It seemed quieter. More subdued. Like they had slowed down.

Sitting up, Grace attempted to look at her watch, but could barely see the white sleeve of her nightgown. She slipped out of the covers, crept to the window and held her arm at just the appropriate angle to get a reading from the faint moon's offering. In the process, she noticed that the moonlight seemed muffled by a shroud of fog. 12:30. If her eyes were reading correctly, she had been asleep for a couple of hours. Certainly, it was too late for helping Paden. The theft of the silver would have been attempted by now. Crall was in a hurry for some reason.

Grace had to move. She closed the curtains of her bed. Should her father wake, he would not see her gone and assume she was behind them. Squeaking through her room door to the hallway, Grace made her way to the Music Room. Her destination would be down to the purser's office. She was fortunate that the deck seemed empty. Most, if not all passengers were off to bed. Even crewmen were noticeably absent. As she ran to the main staircase, she reached for her necklace to keep it from bouncing, as she always did when she ran. It was then she realized it had been placed in the safe. Her most prized possession. The safe was probably empty, and she might not see her necklace again. It may have been a clever way of getting her father to reveal the combination, but it was a foolish thing to do, leaving it there.

Sliding her hand down the smooth wooden rail of the staircase, Grace anticipated what she might see outside of the purser's office on Shelter Deck. There were no sounds. No sign of a commotion. As she approached the last set of steps, she saw the two uniformed officers, once again, slumped in their chairs. Were they still on duty, or were they in a forced sleep from Paden's ankle medicine? She cautiously looked under their caps. Out completely. She was going to nudge the officer with the moustache—look for signs of life—when she saw that the purser's office door was open halfway. She crept forward, pushed the door slowly, causing it to creak. The lights had been left on and Grace immediately looked at the safe. Its small, but heavy door was open a crack. Moving quickly now, she bolted to the safe, flung the door open and peered inside. She shouldn't have been surprised. She had been the accomplice. She had given them the key they needed in the form of the combination numbers. Of course, the silver would be completely gone. *They actually did it,* she realized, shaking her head.

Now that it was done, she began to feel remorse. Perhaps, deep inside, she thought it wouldn't work. That somehow, the job would be compromised. Maybe her weariness, before her sleep, had compromised her ethical capacity. But, now it was too late. Even the fire bells on the bridge were silent. Paden's failsafe distraction had not been necessary. The caper went off without a hitch. *What have I done?*

She stormed out of the office door and had one intent. She had to do the only thing that she could think of that would save Paden. It was risky. He would hate her for it. But, she had to do it. She would have to squeal on him. Tell the authorities that he was in trouble. Perhaps, by his own design. Yet, he needed intervention. Grace would have to find the one man that could help her. Paden's father. He had to be somewhere about the First Class decks. She would find him. Find him now.

But, find him where? This was a big ship. She had just come from the Upper Promenade Deck. She hadn't seen him there, although she only visited a small portion of that deck. She decided to poke her head into the First Class Dining Saloon, since she was right there. The lights were almost completely dimmed. The room that she dined in earlier, so full of food, folks, music, and clanking dishes, was now quieter than a cemetery. The only noise evident was the slow hum of the ship's engines beneath her feet. There was no point in searching here.

She turned her attention from Shelter Deck to Lower Promenade Deck. She hadn't ventured much on this deck. Making her way up one flight of the staircase, Grace turned right, then cranked her head upward ship, glancing up a portside hallway. No one. She made her way to the opposite end of the staircase and peered up the starboard hall. Still, no one. She turned around to look at doors that appeared to house a First Class lounge. A quick glance through the door's window revealed an emptiness, but Grace gathered that it had been occupied recently as she inhaled some wisps of cigar and pipe vapours.

"Can I—"

Grace jumped. A voice startled her. She turned. It was him—Mr. Steele. "Where did you come from?" she asked, somewhat embarrassed, as she looked at his formal uniform jacket and tie and realized she was adorned in her sleeping attire.

"I might ask the same of you, Ms. Hathaway? Doing a bit of sleepwalking are we? Or, perhaps you are hoping to share a late night cigar with the gentlemen?"

Grace might have appreciated his wit at any other time, but not now, as she was in a hurry. She would have to ask him about Paden's Father. "Have you seen Mr. Thomas, sir?" she asked politely.

"Haven't we already played this game, earlier this evening?" Finding she was not amused, he continued. "Young Mr. Thomas, or Mr. Thomas senior?"

"Assistant Chief Steward. That Mr. Thomas," answered Grace, with definite clarification.

"No. I'm afraid not. He could be anywhere at this point. Perhaps he is chasing down his prodigal son as we speak."

Grace felt uneasy about speaking with Mr. Steele regarding the reason for her search of Paden's father. When Grace first met Paden, he told her that Mr. Steele was after his father's job. That he was bitter about not being promoted himself. She didn't want to give Mr. Steele leverage against Mr. Thomas, as a result of Paden's troubles. She knew that Mr. Steele was already hunting for Paden for being a derelict of his duties, and this might get his father into trouble.

"If you don't mind me saying so, Ms. Hathaway," continued Mr. Steele, "I don't think it is a good idea you being out this late, particularly dressed…" He cleared his throat. "Or, shall I say, not quite dressed."

He had a point. Grace should have put her dress back on. If

Harriet could see her now, she would pitch a high scream and have a colossal tantrum. However, thinking upon this made Grace care even less at this point.

"Listen, Grace," spoke Mr. Steele in a softer tone. "I'm concerned for you. You seem to be anxious about something. Is there anything I can assist you with?"

"What makes you think that?" she asked, but then realized it was a stupid question. *Here I am, wandering the ship, dressed for bed, late at night, while most passengers are asleep. The obvious question from Mr. Steele would be, 'Why can't she wait until the morning?'*

He looked her over. "Just a hunch."

She smiled.

"There. I think that's the first time I've seen you smile since you came aboard." He leaned into her a little. "I know it's none of my business, but I can't help but wonder if there is something the matter. Is it your new stepmother?"

Grace was surprised. "How do you know of such things?"

"I overheard your father speaking with her about the upcoming wedding, as they arrived for dinner tonight. I surmised that is why you must be so bothered. It must be a difficult thing, really. She seems to be quite a…" He stopped himself, and changed thoughts. "It's really none of my business. I'm sorry."

Grace wanted to know what he was going to say. "It's all right. Don't be sorry." She couldn't help herself. Mr. Steele had somehow intuitively read Grace like a book. He seemed to know her situation, and empathized with her. He was warm, and she might even say charming. *He may be after Mr. Thomas' job, but he might deserve it*, she thought. *He cares about the needs of the passengers.*

"I should say 'goodnight,' Grace. I hope you find Mr. Thomas. If I see him, I shall let him know you were looking for him, as I hope you will extend the same courtesy to me." He slowly turned to leave.

Grace thought for a brief moment. "Wait, Mr. Steele. There's..." she hesitated for a second, but then plunged herself in. "There's something I need to tell you. It's about Paden Thomas. He's committed a terrible mistake, and he desperately needs our help."

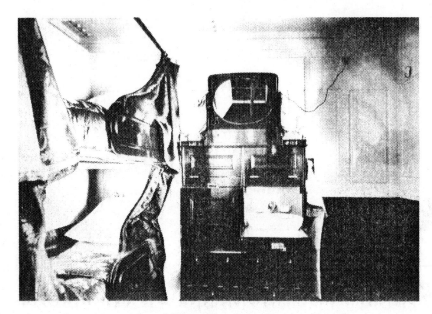

A First Class Stateroom

Chapter 9

"What has Mr. Thomas done this time?" questioned Mr. Steele, with a tone that might be used when correcting a defiant schoolboy.

"He has gotten mixed up with a bad lot. He has stolen something valuable. Something very valuable," confessed Grace.

"You mean, like some money or jewellery?" pressed Mr. Steele.

"No. Much more valuable. He and his people have stolen—"

Steele finished her sentence. "The silver? No. It's not possible." He looked to Grace for confirmation from her expression and appeared shocked at her wide eyes and gaping mouth. "Come with me," he said, leading Grace towards the staircase. Following a hasty descent of her boots down the grand staircase, then a quick step across the carpet to the office, Grace and Mr. Steele arrived at the sleeping officers.

Mr. Steele stole a glance at the two men, slouched in their chairs, but then he focused on the office. He pushed the door open. Before Grace could get in, Mr. Steele stormed out and collided with her, almost knocking her over.

"Wake up, you!" scolded Mr. Steele to one of the officers. No response. He looked at the other, and tried the same. Nothing. "Listen, Grace. What do you know about this theft?"

Grace struggled for words, and nothing came out.

"Grace, you must tell me. There is much at stake here," he said to her with glaring eyes.

Grace tried to speak. "It was only tonight, that I..."

Mr. Steele put his hands on her arms and gently rubbed them, as though they were the access point to the information.

"Paden told me about the plot to steal the silver, only hours ago. I didn't want to help, but they..." She stopped because she felt her voice starting to crack. It would soon be a weeping tone.

"Listen, Grace. No one blames you. Just tell me where they are...so I can help Mr. Thomas."

Grace felt that she should comply. She already entrusted her secret with Mr. Steele, and it would be too hard to turn that ship around. "I will tell you everything, but please, don't arrest Paden. He isn't the one you need to arrest. He is only being used by Crall."

"Crall!" repeated Mr. Steele, looking away in thought. "I should have known. He works at the heart of the ship. He's been here for years. He would know everything about this ship."

"Then, if I help you, you will see to it that Paden is not harmed in any way?"

Mr. Steele focused on Grace again, this time, softening his eyes on hers, and not allowing them to wander. Even though he seemed at least ten years her senior, she couldn't help but be attracted to his sensitivity.

"Listen to me, Grace. What you did here, telling me about all this, was a very brave thing. Mr. Thomas...Paden...is very lucky to have a friend like you. I promise you, no harm will come to him. It is the real mastermind of such a selfish plot that I would like to punish. And that also, is a promise."

Grace smiled in assurance that there would be enough time to turn events around and avoid a disastrous outcome. "What should I do, Mr. Steele?" she asked.

"Who else knows about this, Grace?"

"No one. That is, only those directly involved, and myself. And I don't even know who all is part of it."

"Good," said Mr. Steele with a smile. "Here is what I would like you to do." What followed was a series of instructions that involved her speaking to no one, making her way down to the engine room and meeting Mr. Steele there. He would need her to show him exactly where the bars were being kept, so that he could have certain proof in arresting Crall.

Grace didn't relish the thought of returning to the inner stomach of the ship, as it was like being dared to step into a house that was haunted. Yet, she wanted to make sure Paden was safe, and that she could retrieve her necklace, assuming that Paden, or one of the others, had taken it. She had been having trouble remembering exactly what her mother looked like, and it pained her to be separated from the last vestige of her mother's appearance. She would do whatever it took to get the picture back.

She started to move, keeping in mind a series of staircases that Mr. Steele had directed her to. She wouldn't have to risk bumping into crewmembers in the galley, or the remains of entertainment holdouts from any of the lounges. The staircases and hallways would be mostly clear of passengers, who were by this time, being lulled to sleep by the gentle hum of the ship's engines. She moved up a level, and out onto deck. To the aft part of the Lower Promenade Deck, then down the set of stairs she recognized earlier from the trip to the doctor. Across the stern, from starboard to port on Shelter Deck, and down another staircase. At the foot of the stairs, she glanced at a sign that read "Main Deck".

Following Mr. Steele's directions, she proceeded up Main Deck towards the bow.

Grace was amazed at the layout of the ship. On the upper floors, there was no sparing of wood and brass trimmings. As she progressed further below, she noticed that pipes began popping out here and there. Now, she followed them the length of the halls. The wooden panelled walls of the higher decks, complete with paintings, bright trimmings, and brass portholes, were replaced with steel bulkheads and rivets aplenty. After she passed through the Third Class Dining Saloon, she continued moving forward past passenger rooms. She noticed a door open briefly, as a passenger appeared to be shuffling a suitcase under a bed. Pipes and steel also dominated the room, and the bunk looked like a metal cage in comparison to Grace's padded, decorative piece of furniture.

Along the way, she also noticed a couple of large sliding metal doors. She was about to go down another staircase to the next deck below, when she stopped to look back at the last sliding door. Paden had shown her his main responsibility. It was cranking the gear. The gear that closed the watertight door one deck below. She seemed most certain, based on how much distance she had travelled in the direction of the bow, that this must be the door that Paden was responsible for closing. Her concern for him grew. She was hoping that he would still be out of trouble in the morning and able to man that gear, so that he wouldn't disappoint his father.

She descended the final staircase that would lead her to Lower Deck and to the engine room. As she walked back towards the stern, she was reminded of her earlier experience. Darkness abounded. Strange odours permeated the air and infiltrated her lungs. Steam shot out from various structures, and they were frequently decorated with fiery incandescent glowing. Painted men, with rolled sleeves and filthy trousers, shovelled coal from under their feet, in between wiping their blackened brows. It all seemed demonic and reminded Grace of Dante's "Inferno."

She sidestepped her way through workers who gave small glances and raised eyebrows, but otherwise seemed unconcerned that someone from above was lost in their world.

She eventually made her way back to the engine room by passing cargo, pillars, and through more watertight doorways. Entering the massive engine room from the walkways up top, she looked down to see if she could find Paden. Surprisingly, no crewmembers walked the upper walkways. *Crall must have ordered the rest of the crewmen out of the engine room,* she thought, *so that they wouldn't know what was going on.*

Grace could only see three heads below her as she peered around the top of one of the gigantic engines. It was Paden. He was talking with Crall and a uniformed crewman. She looked more intently and noticed that the additional crewman was, in fact, Eddie. He had donned the black uniform jacket and cap, most likely, to pose as one of the officers guarding the silver outside the purser's office. Paden was the other impostor. None of the three men took notice of Grace from above, and she was able to find a ladder to make her way down to their level, without event.

Now down below, Grace moved around the noisy engine to come up behind Crall. Paden and Eddie would be facing her, once she made the turn around the final corner. She stopped. Their voices were getting louder. Despite the loud heartbeat of metal, she heard their raised voices as they struggled to communicate.

"But, when do we get our share?" asked a voice. It had to be Paden's.

"There it is," responded Crall's low, raspy tone.

A mailbag was tossed and landed beside Paden as Grace remained hidden around the corner of the engine. As it landed, it 'clanked'. It would contain silver bars. But, only a few, it seemed.

"How many's in there?" demanded Paden.

"You're lucky to get any," returned Crall.

"You'll get the rest after you help me load the silver onto the Lady Evelyn."

"The Lady Evelyn?" questioned Eddie.

"That's right," answered Crall. "The mail and I have a ship to catch. And you'll do it quickly, or you won't be leaving this engine room alive."

Grace poked one eye around the corner and saw Crall's back, facing Eddie and Paden. She bent down so that they couldn't see her past Crall. Her worst fears were realized. Crall pulled something out of his pocket. It was a revolver. Pointed directly at Eddie and Paden as they stood together.

So that is why Crall was in such a hurry to steal the silver. It didn't make sense to Grace that the silver would be taken at the beginning of the voyage. That would spark a ship-wide search. Even with a clever hiding place, the thieves would not be out of danger. But, Crall had no intention on keeping the silver, or himself, on board. He was using Paden and Eddie.

"But, we had a deal," spoke Paden.

"The plan has changed. Pray that I don't alter it further," spoke Crall waving his revolver towards Paden's face. "Now hurry up. Pick up those bags and start moving them to the lift."

Paden and Eddie glanced at one another, then bent down to grab the drawstrings on the mailbags. They struggled to drag the heavy cargo. In all, there were about eight bags of silver. *No doubt, Crall would use his revolver to gain access on the Lady Evelyn,* thought Grace. *Once aboard, who knows if he would be seen again?* She had to do something. Once Crall was finished with Paden and Eddie, he might try to get rid of them. Shoot them. Or, throw them overboard. She had to intervene.

Looking down, Grace noticed a bright red, metal wrench or tool of some sort. She stooped to pick it up with one hand, but found that she had to bend completely to the metal floor, and pick it up with both hands. Fumbling with the heavy object in the air, she compromised her hidden position behind the engine and approached Crall. Her heels rattled the floor below, and Crall turned towards her, as she was about to pound his skull. In an instant, her plan had failed. He dodged her onetime swing of the weighty tool, as she fell to the floor with the pull. She looked up to see Crall's ugly face and the barrel of the revolver looking down on her.

"Well, hello," he growled. "Look what we have here. It seems we have someone else who wants to help. Sorry. I don't take weak women."

His slight movement of his hand caused Grace to be certain that she was about to be shot in the head. She winced. A loud 'pop' echoed in her ears. He had fired. She felt her head. No pain. No blood. He missed. Just then, Crall's heavy body collapsed on top of her. A painful choke oozed from his lips. He turned limp, and rolled off her. Red hands. She pushed him fully off her, and noticed her hands were bloody from clutching his back. He had been shot in the back.

"Grace. Are you all right?" asked Paden, reaching to help her off the hard, cold floor, along with the assistance of Eddie.

"I think so. What hap—"

Grace looked behind the two young men. Another uniformed officer held a revolver. His officer's cap rose slowly. It was…

"Mr. Steele!" exclaimed an alarmed Grace. She was shaking from the thought of her near-death experience, but managed to find comfort in recognizing her saviour.

"I told you I would get him, Grace," spoke Mr. Steele.

"Steele!" said Paden, in what Grace felt was an unthankful tone. "How did you know we were here?"

"Let's just say," he said calmly, "I had an anonymous tip from a friendly passenger." He made quick eye contact with Grace, divulging her as the tipster.

"Grace?" said Paden, turning to her in disbelief. "I trusted you. I thought you were on my side. Not his!"

She was still shaking, but managed to show her annoyance at Paden. "I did you a favour! You just don't know it yet!" she yelled.

"A favour? Me? By squealin' to 'im!"

"It's all right, Paden. Mr. Steele is going to help us," said Grace.

"Are you sure about that?" spoke Eddie for the first time since Steele's arrival.

Grace looked across to Eddie, who only made eye contact with Steele. She was not sure what he was implying. That is, until she looked back to Steele. His revolver remained raised, and pointed. Pointed at the three of them.

"Thank you Grace, for helping me solve this terrible crime," he said.

"Mr. Steele?" questioned Grace.

"Well, I should first thank my partner, Mr. Crall. He proved to be most useful. But, not anymore it seems," he said laughing at the floor where Crall's lifeless body lay spilling blood.

"You were working for Crall?" asked Grace.

"Are you serious?" he said angrily. "He was working for me. Do you really think someone of his ogre brain could come up with a plot such as this? He only kept me informed. He told me of your hesitation to help us. That is why I had to slip that note under your door, to convince you to follow through, for Paden's sake."

"So, it was you?" said Grace to Steele.

"I told you, Grace," interrupted Paden. "I told you there were other people working in this. People that we didn't even know about. I never trusted him," he said pointing at Steele with a scowl. "And you never should have, either."

Grace felt defeated. Paden was right. She had fallen so easily for the belief that Crall was the mastermind. *What was the number one rule of mystery books?* she thought to herself. *The culprit is always the person that is least likely to have done it.* How she had forgotten to rely on her own reading experience. Steele seemed so concerned about ship rules. Seemed concerned for the silver's safety. Seemed so concerned about Grace's well-being. She should have seen it coming. She was a fool. And now her mistake could cost lives. Her life, as well as those of her new friends, Eddie and Paden.

"And now, gentlemen," spoke Steele, "I have an appointment with a Lady, and I don't want to be late. You'll be helping me load those bags. And don't worry," he said, turning to Grace, "I rather fancy a woman doing a man's job."

Steele was planning the same escape as Crall. Perhaps, he had been using Crall all along, with the intent of killing him.

Paden stepped towards Steele, causing Steele to redirect the aim of his revolver to Paden, alone. Paden stopped moving and spoke. "We're not going to help you, or anyone move this silver."

Steele's face grew red for a moment, but softened to a smile, as his fingers danced on the revolver. "All right, then. This is how we handle mutiny aboard this ship." He raised the revolver slightly higher and pointed it at Paden's chest. He hesitated, then, redirected aim at Eddie.

"No!" cried Paden, pushing forward and rushing to Eddie, but not in time. A single 'pop' was heard, as before. Eddie clutched his chest and fell back into Paden's arms.

"Eddie!" cried Grace. She assisted Paden, who fell to the floor with Eddie in his lap. "You murderer!" she screamed. Tears now flowed freely, and she slowly stood, more blood on her hands and robe. She looked at her hands, then down at Eddie. He was lifeless, just like Crall. *He didn't deserve this. He was a good man. A faithful friend.*

She didn't think anymore, but lunged at Steele. Another echo of a shot rang through the loose acoustics of the mighty ceiling. But, it was unlikely to be heard by anyone above the engine noise, and she and the others remained visually sheltered from any crewmembers by the engine. Grace didn't stop and check herself for injury, but knocked Steele enough that the revolver fell from his hand, banging on a metal grating below, and slipping about a foot underneath. He struggled to pick it out, but it was just out of reach, and Grace distracted him further, by grabbing his head with her hand. She clawed his face. She forced her fingers into his eyes, gouging and intruding his sockets enough that he submitted the reach for the revolver and screamed in pain.

"Come on, Grace. Let's get out of here!" yelled Paden, as he grabbed Grace's arm and flung her to her feet.

"What about Eddie?" she asked, looking down.

"He's gone. He's gone."

She looked into Paden's eyes. She trusted him enough that he knew best at this point. She took his hand to leave. He stopped, picked up the mailbag that was thrown by Crall. It contained only a few bars. Grace was surprised he would take it at this point, considering his friend had just died over it. She felt that he must still be clinging to the hope of its use. Perhaps this small package would be a healthy impetus to his future apart from this ship. One thing was for certain: they couldn't drag all the silver.

They looked back and saw Steele floundering on the ground in shouts of pain. They stormed away from the engine room, Paden with a 'clinking' mailbag in tow, and raced up the Lower Deck.

"Where are we going? What is your plan?" asked Grace in between strides up the darkened deck.

"Plan? I don't really 'ave one yet. I'm just kinda' makin' it up as we go."

"Oh, dear. That is not good."

"No, it isn't," returned Paden.

They continued running, until Grace could run no more in her heels. "Wait. Rest," she insisted.

"We 'ave to get somewhere out of sight," said Paden looking around at the various coal workers they had been passing. "Steele's likely to make it back up top and get his men on us. Who knows what he is capable of? I still can't believe he killed poor Eddie. It's all my fault. I should never 'ave gotten' him mixed into this."

Grace focused on the task at hand and thought for a moment. "What if we go back on the upper decks, and hide somewhere up top, say on the Boat Deck? It's dark outside, and no passengers are out at this late hour. It's unlikely Steele will look there."

"We can duck under a lifeboat, or beside a funnel," said Paden, building on her idea. "We should get to the bridge anyway, to warn the captain about Steele."

"Or warn your father, Paden."

He hesitated, but gave in. "Yes. Or Father."

The two climbed the staircase and made their way up to Main Deck. They continued to follow a similar route as Grace's from moments ago, but Paden showed Grace some shortcuts through areas that were restricted to crewmembers. He stopped at one point.

"What is it?" Grace asked.

"There's something I have to do first," he replied.

"But, we must hide."

"We will. But, first…" He took Grace up to the Upper Deck. He led her to the bow, near the children's playground known as the pit. He ducked under the small, hinged door that gave access to the children to enter the sand pit. Only hours ago, was he leaning against the rail, speaking with the parents of the little girl. "I just 'ave to hide these." He took the mailbag of silver, placed it in a shallow grave that he quickly dug with his bare hands.

Grace was feeling annoyed. Eddie had just died for this silver, and Paden was persistent in keeping it. "Is that really necessary, right now?" she asked, with no attempt to hide her disgusted tone.

Paden didn't respond. Once finished the burial, he hopped the fence rail. "Let's go," he said. She continued on with him. They made it up the decks without any incident. No passengers roamed, for it was now 12:48 a.m. by her watch. Scattered crewmembers could be seen in the hallways, off in the distance, taking care of their own overnight duties, whatever they may be.

Finally arriving onto Upper Promenade Deck and heading outdoors, Grace didn't find the cool air threatening for the moment. She had perspired from all the movement and was relieved to have the droplets of sweat blown away from her face.

"Let's go up 'ere," said Paden, guiding Grace to the staircase where he staged his earlier fall. She noticed him limping slightly as he led her by the hand. This time, she believed he must have genuinely hurt his ankle in the flight for freedom from below. They headed immediately for cover between the two ship's funnels, towards the rear funnel, where there were two storage tanks of some kind. They collapsed to the deck floor in between, where they were sheltered from sight, from sound, and from air.

They stared across at one another briefly, as they both leaned against a tank and panted rapidly.

"What now…Paden?" forced Grace with difficulty.

"Don't know…have to think."

After a few moments, Paden perched his head high and looked around, as though he noticed something unusual.

"What is it?" asked Grace.

"We're slowing down. You 'ear it? The engines. Slowing. We must be meeting up with the Lady Evelyn. I s'pose Steele's goin' to miss his evening rendezvous with his Lady."

"Let's only hope," said Grace.

"But, we shouldn't count him out, just yet."

"I agree."

Paden rose to his feet, and Grace followed his lead. He looked up at the sky. "It's so calm, tonight," he said.

At that comment, Grace realized that the cool breeze had disappeared. Perhaps, it was because the ship had nearly come to a full stop. She gazed upward. The stars flittered in the sky. It seemed such a paradox to her that it was so peaceful now, standing here under nature's glorious ceiling, amidst murder, and the threat of more deaths to come.

"Let's check out what's 'appening," said Paden, as he stepped away from their quiet solace of the funnels and made his way towards the lifeboats, then to the starboard side railing.

Grace followed, but cautiously turned her glance up and down the deck. Standing between two lifeboats, she assumed that they were still well hidden from anyone. She now turned her attention downward towards a small vessel that cast minimal light on the hull of the Empress, in cooperation with the new moon's glimmer, several decks down. The water was so peaceful that she could hear individual voices talking, as several bags were thrown from one of the Empress' gangway doors, onto the deck of the tiny ship. She couldn't make out any words, but felt that the tones were cheery enough that neither of the men was Steele. The exchange happened quickly and without incident. The ship slipped into the darkness of the river, and faded from Grace's line of sight.

As the Empress' engines began to rumble once again, Grace came to an obvious revelation. "Steele. The engine room. Crall. And Eddie."

"What do you mean?" asked Paden.

She had just enough light to read his confused expression. "Don't you see? The engines. They stopped. Then, they started again. The engine room is receiving the captain's commands. Someone is down there doing their job. Someone must have found Crall or Eddie lying there. Maybe they even found Steele."

"But, we haven't heard an alarm? Then, that must mean…"

Grace continued. "That must mean that Steele has hidden the bodies from the crewmen there, and is still alive. Otherwise, they would have found the bodies and alerted the bridge by now."

Paden glanced up deck towards the extremely, faint light emanating from the bridge windows at the side. "No action there to tell about," he said. "Maybe, Steele's tryin' to keep things secret. Handle it his own way."

"What do we do, then? Go to the bridge?"

"Not sure," said Paden. He walked back to the funnel section. "It's Steele's move now. Until we can be sure what he will do, I suggest we stay 'ere for now."

"Here?" questioned Grace with uncertainty. "You mean…all night?"

"Well, if not for all night…part of the night. I just need to think. And I'm too tired right now." He walked towards some lights shining upwards from a section of the floor between the funnels.

"What is this place?" asked Grace, looking down on the lit area below.

"It's the skylight, above the Music Room," answered Paden.

"Only, it doesn't seem to be giving off any music tonight." He collapsed on the hard deck floor and slouched. "I can't believe he's gone. It should 'ave been me lying down there in the engine room."

"You tried to stop it," said Grace attempting to comfort Paden.

"I never should have involved him," he continued, shaking his lowered head.

You never should have involved anyone, including yourself, Grace thought, but didn't mention it, as she felt it wouldn't help the situation at this point.

Grace joined Paden on the floor. They sat side by side in silence for a few moments. She was at a loss for words. Finally, Paden broke the silence.

"How did you do that back there, anyway?"

"Do what?" she answered.

"Attack Steele. He's a pretty big man. You gouged his eyes pretty bad, he couldn't get up. Where'd ya' get the strength to do that?"

"Ten years of piano lessons," she answered with a small, sensitive grin.

"I see," was the reply. Paden laid back and rested his head on the vibrating floor.

Grace looked down at the lit windows of the vacant room. *The music inside of me has gone silent, too,* she thought. She followed Paden's lead, and lay her head down. *What am I doing here?* she thought. She should be in her cabin, sound asleep. In fact, she desired to be at home in her own bed. Free of worry. But what she desired was irrelevant. She thought of the events of the day. Everyone seemed to be full of desires for what cannot be. Her father wished for her to happily accept a new life and a new mother. Paden desired a second chance of a family, living together in England. Crall and Steele both hungrily wanted the wealth of possessing that silver. *Sometimes, the desires of one's heart can never be—no matter how much we work for them*, she thought.

Grace's eyelids grew heavy. She tried forcing them open, but a voice inside her told her to let go. She knew that falling asleep might lead to capture and death at the hands of Steele—but she didn't have the strength to reason it out. She would have to resign herself to whatever might happen. *Let go. Let...*

Men working in one of the many coal bunkers

Chapter 10

"Go," urged Grace's father, motioning her to the front of the room. Grace couldn't bear glancing at Andrew's body in the open casket. It was horror enough watching him drown, but looking into his lifeless face would wound her eternally. *What would he look like? Would his face be discoloured? Would he look artificial?*

She had seen her mother after she died. It wasn't pleasant, but she needed closure. She needed to know that it wasn't an empty box being laid into the ground. Or, that she was still alive, trying to get out of the casket, after it had been covered in eight feet of dirt.

She had to do it. Inching her way to the front of the funeral chapel, Grace first saw his black suit jacket. Her gaze followed his buttons up to his necktie. She had to do it. She had to stare into his face. See Andrew one last time.

Two long blasts. Two loud, long blasts. She turned to look at the organist who signalled the beginning of the ceremony with a chord of such haunting dissonance. She turned back to the casket, but two figures blocked her view of the opening. The lid was shut.

"No!" she shouted. "I'm not ready. I wasn't finished."

They ignored her. She stormed the casket and pushed them

aside to force the lid open. The two black suits grabbed her by the arms to subdue her.

"No!" she continued. "It's not fair!"

The organist slammed down the keys in two more sustained, persistent loud tones.

"Grace! Are you all right?"

Of course not, she thought. She was cold. It was dark. She sat up. It was night. On the Empress. She had fallen asleep on the Boat Deck.

"Are you all right, Grace?" asked Paden, who had subdued her by the arms.

"Yes. I think so."

"You scared me. Must 'ave been quite the dream," he said.

"I'm…fine," she said, as she looked around in the darkness, still attempting to regain focus on the situation. "What is happening?"

"Not sure," said Paden. "Something's up. Something strange. I think there is another ship nearby, but I can't see a thing."

Grace stood and looked around. Something was different. "We've stopped," she said.

"Yes. I know."

"You said earlier, that we had to drop off the pilot. At Father Point, wasn't it?"

"We've already done that, about thirty minutes ago."

"What time is it now?" she inquired.

"Just shy of 2 a.m.," he answered, holding his wrist immediately in front of his eyes, struggling to read his wristwatch.

It's quiet, she thought. *The ship's engines are dead. No sound of water hitting the hull. But, something else is different.* She looked around, but couldn't make out any shoreline. There weren't any ship's lights out in the distance. *Why does Paden think there is a ship out there?* It was then, she realized why she couldn't see past the arc-shaped beams that secured the lifeboats, over by the railing. It was fog. Heavy fog. So thick, that it would choke the brightest of lights, only feet from the side of the vessel.

"There's been several blasts of the ships' whistles. Ours and hers," said Paden. "She's out there, somewhere. The captain signalled with two long blasts. That's maritime signal for 'all stop'. So the other vessel would know our intention." He moved away from Grace, stepped down and away from their funnel hideaway, and moved towards the Boat Deck railing.

Two long blasts, thought Grace. *That explains my overzealous organist.*

"Paden, wait," said Grace, as she mimicked his movements. She didn't want to be alone in the eerie silence of the grey sky. She moved against the railing, in between two lifeboats, and held onto a rope that dangled down from the rigging. She wanted something tangible to hold onto. Something for security. What was out there? Nothing. It was silent. Yet, she couldn't let go and walk away. She spoke not a word to Paden. He too, remained silent in a trance. He panted, looked out into nothing but a charcoal wall of uncertainty.

"Not right," spoke Paden, after a few moments silence. He was standing on the first rung of the metal railing, to gain a better vantage point over the deck. But, there was nothing to see a foot away that wasn't visible on Grace's side of the railing. "It's," he continued, "not right. There's…"

"What?" asked Grace, looking at Paden's obsessed glare into the anomaly.

Three hasty blasts were heard from the ship's whistle.

"Oh, blimy!" shouted Paden, grasping his hands to his head, and still staring out into the unknown.

"What is it?" asked Grace. "Why did the Empress blow—"

"It wasn't the Empress! That was another ship! Out there! She was giving the backing signal! I think she's heading directly for us."

Grace tightened her grip on the rope. Looking at Paden, he stared into her eyes for the first time in moments. He had the look of a madman. He looked away again.

"There!" he yelled, and pointed off the starboard railing.

Grace turned to look away from Paden, and back into the darkness. She could faintly see water below, gentle waves lapping over one another. As she looked slightly higher, she noticed a faint light. It was red. Then another. Green. Then, white. It slowly became brighter. It moved towards them. Then, she saw it. A bow of a ship. A large ship, but lower to the water. It would hit them in seconds, almost directly below the point where she and Paden stood. She froze. She couldn't believe it would happen. It couldn't. It had to be a mistake. It would miss. But, it would have to be a near miss. During her rationalization, she looked at Paden. He didn't move.

"Paden," she said. "Paden. Paden!" she said, increasing her voice's intensity. "We have to move, Paden!" The large ship was upon them. It didn't turn, like she thought it would. Its massive hull pointed directly at them. She jumped back and bumped into a wall. She lost sight of the ship as she collapsed backwards to the floor.

"No way," uttered Paden, still clinging to the rail.

A yell. Paden fell. Tripped over something. Fell backwards. A giant storm of fiery yellow sparks danced up to his feet, and over his body. Steel upon steel. Sharp, squealing. The sparks teased Paden for an instant, then moved down the deck to search for others. The floor they stood upon had risen up several feet.

"Paden!" yelled Grace, as she felt the ship slowly subside back down to its normal position. She rushed to him. "Are you all right? What happened?"

Paden scrambled to his feet, and grabbed hold of the hard, wood rail. He bent over the railing to survey the damage to the hull. He flew back. He looked up the deck towards the bridge. It was the captain. His lit, shadowlike silhouette was frozen as he stood looking over the starboard rail outside of the open door, leading from the bridge. He yelled through a megaphone at the other ship. "Keep ahead! Keep going ahead on your engines!"

Yes, of course, thought Grace. *Keep the hole plugged. That's what he's trying to do.*

The captain continued yelling towards the phantom ship, then noticed Paden and Grace's figures positioned down the deck.

"Captain!" yelled Paden. "Massive breach of the hull!" He stretched over the railing again. "Through Orlop, Lower, and Upper Decks! Floodin' is imminent!"

The captain disappeared. No doubt, to spring into some sort of plan.

Grace turned towards the stern to see the ghost ship's lights disappear into the fog, away from the Empress. "Paden. What do we do?" asked Grace, trembling in her nightclothes.

"We 'ave to..."

A loud siren was heard. Grace shrieked at the awful noise. It sounded danger. It sounded panic. It sounded disaster.

"We need to get below deck. Warn people. That size of carving will bring us down in no time," spoke Paden quickly, but plainly into Grace's eyes.

"Down?"

"Yes. We're going under. No doubt about it."

Grabbing Grace by the excess material on her robe sleeve, Paden dragged her to the staircase. Skipping several steps on the way down, he led her to the deck door that was closest to her room. Flinging the door open, the two pounced inside the doors.

Hallways were barren. The siren could be heard, but not in an alarming fashion as outside.

"Where is everybody?" asked Grace in bewilderment.

"They're all asleep. We've got to wake 'em," demanded Paden. He bolted to doors and began pounding with his fists until he shrunk them away in pain. Then he kicked.

"Wake up! The ship is sinking!" she yelled. She felt silly, alone in the hall with Paden. Certainly, it had to be a mistake. Maybe Paden had overstated their doom. He had been unreliable already. She didn't want people angry with her for nothing. Their salvation, however, seemed more important than her embarrassment.

A few heads poked out of the cabins. "What the—?" spoke a man with a moustache.

"The ship's been hit. She's sinking!" yelled Grace.

The man was in a daze. He closed his door. Then, opened it. "What?" he asked again.

Grace and Paden were frustrated at the apathetic response. People were in need of saving, yet they were asleep. She had to do something more productive. "Father," she said. "I have to wake Father." Running the short distance to her room, she heard Paden call back to her.

"Grace. After you fetch your father, head to the lifeboats!"

"What? Where are you going?" she asked.

"I have something I 'ave to do. Below deck."

"Below deck? You're leaving me? To go below deck? The water is flooding the lower decks by now. You can't."

He turned away and looked at the staircase leading down. Then, back at her. "Just get to the lifeboats." He disappeared behind the wall. Grace ran back and caught a glimpse of his back as he hit the bottom step and turned. Disappeared.

Grace didn't have time to waste. She ran back to her cabin.

Forcing the door open, she fumbled for the electric light switch. Running and jumping at her father's bed, she yelled, "Father!" His head didn't move. She grabbed his bedclothes. Flat. There was nothing under them. He was gone.

Bolting out of the room, Grace collided with something in the doorway, causing her to fall backwards onto the floor. She clutched her forehead in pain. She had left the door open. What was it?

"Grace? Where have you been?" demanded a woman's voice. It was Harriet. Winifred stood behind in the hall.

"Where's Father? The ship. It's sinking!"

"You stupid fool," said Harriet. "Your father has left. Gone. Looking for you down below."

"Down below?"

"Yes. He said there was a collision. Another ship. Said we better get to the lifeboats. He left us, because you weren't in your cabin. He feared you were off with that young man. Below deck. How could you?"

"Below deck?" repeated Grace, in a daze, still clutching her throbbing forehead. "I have to find him. It's all my fault. I have to get him, before—"

"Yes, it is your fault," scolded Harriet. "Inconveniencing your father by your silly ways. You should be…"

Grace didn't hear Harriet's remaining words. Only mumblings. *Does she not realize the severity of the situation? The essence of time.* She thrust her arms forward, sending Harriet into the door, its frame flying backwards as it swung on the hinges. She climbed over Harriet's clumsy fallen body and past Winifred's frozen wide-eyed stare as the servant backed herself into the corner wall of the hallway in fear.

"It's all my fault," she repeated, as she ran towards the stairway that Paden had just descended. She passed several passengers who now realized the reality of the evening, and emerged as sober souls, pounding on doors, and donning lifebelts. Two eager men bounced out of their rooms at precisely the same moment, colliding with one another and falling back. In any other setting, it might be a parody.

Grace focused back on the task at hand. She didn't know where to look for Paden. And, finding her father on this ship would not be easy. *It might not happen*, she feared. But, she didn't have time for pessimism. She ran down the staircase, missing several stairs. As she hit the bottom, the heel of her boots caught an edge of the final step, causing her right ankle to twist. She shrieked in pain as her body was levelled to the floor. Clutching her ankle, she pulled away her boot and tossed it. The ankle didn't sense any relief. She clutched the other foot, and sent the boot flying in another direction. The pain in her ankle was intense, but she didn't have the luxury of healing time. She had to keep moving.

She moved along Lower Promenade Deck. Again, there were only scattered passengers moving from their rooms, some asking for lifebelts. Some remained unaware of the severity of their situation, as Grace overheard one man in an English accent ask, "Hey, chums. Has anyone seen a maroon garment bag?"

Grace noticed a steward frantically knocking on doors, and in some cases, pushing them open and forcing his way in to warn the weary travellers. Word was beginning to spread that time was expiring.

The ship floor lurched upwards slightly, as it did when the other ship had first collided. Grace was already imbalanced because of her wounded foot, and fell into the wall with her hands. She was able to support herself enough to stay standing, and limp on. She called out. "Father! Father! Are you there?" Rising voices dampened her cries.

Moving across to the port side, she came to another staircase, leading down below. She thought she should try another deck. She was feeling frustrated, because all she had time to do was guess and make random hits at various locations of the intricate ship layout. If she guessed wrong, it could be fatal. While most passengers who were awakened were probably heading up to the lifeboats, she was heading in the opposite direction—down.

From the bottom of the staircase, she pushed through a set of doors. She hobbled through the vacant First Class Dining Saloon, and up Shelter Deck, towards the bow. *No sign of him.* As she passed cabins, she pounded her fists on random doors. She didn't have time for them all. Dragging herself forward, she saw more stewards waking other passengers.

She hit another set of stairs heading down. *Father, please be near,* she thought. As she carefully nursed her ankle down the metal stairs, she decided for herself that this had to be her cut-off point. She couldn't go any deeper, or it would be suicide. She would continue the search on her way back up.

Stepping out from the staircase, she realized she was familiar with this location. It led to the children's playground area, the place where she had met up with, and spoken to Paden. Several passengers emerged from behind doors and gave her concerned looks as they hurried by. She read 'Where are you going? Are you crazy?' from their silent faces. Some clutched small suitcases, while others gripped their spouses.

It was then, that Grace noticed a figure ahead, in the large open area that merged with the hallway of cabins. He stood by the sandpit, known as the Garden. It was a man, in uniform. He jumped the short fence and plunged down into the sand. It was Paden. "Paden!" she yelled.

He turned to look at her, as she stood in the edge of the hallway. A flash. Grace looked away to the overhead light. It flickered quickly, sounded a pulsing 'buzz', like a bee, sporadically flying close to and away from one's ear. All went black. Paden had disappeared from view. The walls had disappeared. Holding her hand in front of her face, Grace could see nothing.

A calm drill contrasts the scramble for lifebelts after the collision.

Chapter 11

Falling. She held her hands out to grab whatever might support her. The ship had tossed her on her side. She scrambled for the wall, but was deceived. The wall was not where it should be, but seemed closer to the floor. Reaching to stand again, her bare feet were able to better read the floor than her boots would have. The floor was now slightly angled. She was running out of time to find her father.

"Paden! What are you doing?" she called into the darkness.

A faint light appeared. An emergency light. It paled in comparison to the usual hallway lights, but it was a beacon of salvation now. She looked back up the deck.

"Get out of here, Grace! Save yourself!"

"I'm looking for—"

The walls lurched to the side again. An explosion caused Grace to scream. She watched in horror as a wall of white, foamy water attacked Paden. The flow jostled him. Now, it set a collision course directly to her, hitting her just below the waist as she stood at the entrance to the hallway.

Rising to her toes to elevate herself as high as she could, she immediately thought of the water hole where she had been swimming with Andrew. She had always thought that the river water near her town was cold. But, this was lethal. Enough to cause her to think of giving in and going back up the stairs. *Turn and leave*, she thought to herself. *While there's time*. But, that wouldn't suffice. She had to find her father. Let him know she was still alive. She didn't want him to die for her. She didn't deserve it.

A door beside Grace opened partially, as though it was fighting the current that was climbing its door handle. A man appeared. A child in his arms. He forced the door open, using his body as a human prying tool. "Please," he pleaded to Grace. "Take my child."

Grace sloshed her legs towards the man, read the intent in his eyes, then reached her arms forward. Before she could complete the exchange herself, the young girl jumped to her, clutching her so tightly around the neck that even if Grace let go, the girl would remain attached.

"My wife," the man said, stepping out of the doorway, "she went to the ladies' lavatory. I have to find her. Please. Take my child to safety."

Grace forced the child away from her face enough to look at the girl's tremulous features. It was her. The girl from the playground. The girl Paden treated to dessert.

"Will you do it?" he said, pressing for an answer as he looked in the direction of Paden.

"I will," she said.

"I love you, Anna," he said, kissing the child's forehead and turning away. He disappeared into darkness, several feet away.

Grace looked to Paden again. He was nowhere. He had disappeared. Did the current take him? Was he pinned under something? She bounced her gaze in several directions. *I can't wait*, she thought.

Suddenly, a figure appeared out of the water, near where the sandpit had been. It was Paden. He immediately plunged face down into the water and disappeared again.

"Paden!" she shouted, although he most likely did not hear from under the water. "What is he doing?" she said to herself, as she felt the girl moan and cling tighter. It was then, she realized. *What a fool! He's going for his precious silver. People are dying.*

He surfaced again. *Certainly, the sand and the silver would have been swept away by now,* she thought. At that point, she noticed a coarse feeling around her legs. Reaching down, she scooped some water up to her face. It was gritty and left behind a residue of dark, wet sand, once the water fell away. "Paden!" she yelled again.

This time, he halted his downward movement into the water, stood straight, and looked at her. His chest rose and fell quickly as he heaved for air. She could tell by his conflicted look that he was determined, yet indecisive. He took a step towards her, but then turned his head back to where he started.

"Paden," she said, this time trying to speak calmly. The floor rumbled again below her, causing the girl to scream in Grace's ear. *Certainly, he would respond to the cries of this young one,* she thought. Then, she remembered some important words. "Paden," she said stepping toward him, as water attempted to resist her thigh movement. She was close enough to look into his irrational eyes and speak. "Time is an unstoppable wave that rolls over us all."

He fixed his eyes on Grace. Then on the girl. Then on Grace. He slowly nodded. He understood. The words of his father after his sister's death. He would not gamble time against another young girl's life. He sprang away from his immediate area. "Let's get out of here," he said.

Grace turned, as she moved with the current, back in the direction from which she had come. Little Anna was beginning to become burdensome. Grace didn't know whether she would be able to carry her all the way up to safety, especially with the added burden of unpredictable tremors and angling of the ship's structure. She turned back to ask Paden for assistance. He was not directly behind her, but stood several feet back. He was staring at something. It was a lever. She stopped again. She remembered it as the gear to the watertight door, directly below. It was Paden's responsibility. He had to wind the gear to shut the watertight doors.

"The key is already attached. Someone has started, but left," he said.

"Is it too late to close the door?" asked Grace.

"I'm not sure. But, I have to try anyway." He grabbed the t-bar, and began rotating the gear. Once he started, he settled into a fast sequence. Clutch. Spin. Clutch. Spin. Clutch. Spin. He repeated for about twenty seconds, then stopped.

"What's wrong?" asked Grace.

"I'm cold. I can't feel my hands."

"Maybe we should go. I'm afraid we'll be trapped."

"Paden!" called an approaching voice from across the corridor.

"Mr. Thomas!" said Grace. She was surprised to see Paden's father here. Surely, someone of his high status would be doing high priority evacuation activities above. He still looked official in his buttoned tunic and straightened cap, despite the rushing water, tugging at his trousers.

"Paden," spoke Mr. Thomas, looking at him, then noticing Grace and the little girl. "You need to get out now."

Paden seemed to be surveying his father's face. His father must have been the person who aligned the key on the gear before Paden arrived. *Was he disappointed Paden wasn't there on time? Was he upset?* Grace wondered.

"Father. I need to close the door. Or, is it too late?" asked Paden, sincerely.

"No, son. It's not too late."

Grace might have been too sentimental for her own good, but she was reading double meaning into this exchange of words. Perhaps, it wasn't too late for them—for mutual respect and love.

"Then, I will stay and—"

"No," he insisted. "You have a greater responsibility now," he said, looking at Grace and Anna, and gently rubbing Anna's arm. Grace was touched by his compassion and gentleness. Such contrast to what she had witnessed of him up until this point. Tragedy had exposed the heart of his true character.

Paden nodded in understanding. "But, what about the door?"

"I'll take your place," he said, clutching Paden's arm.

The two men were locked in a mutual stare that seemed to last for minutes, although it was most likely seconds. It seemed to Grace, that the two were saying 'goodbye', yet neither acknowledged that kind of finality.

"Father," started Paden. His lips began trembling. His face contorted into a baby's cry. A tear dropped.

"Son," said his father, clutching Paden's neck and drawing his child towards his face in an embrace. They locked for a few seconds, but time would not permit much more.

"Look to your mother. Now, get out of here, before it's too late." He immediately went back to work on the gear, his eyes now focused downward on the task at hand. The water had risen almost to the top of the gear. It was most likely meaningless at this point, but he continued.

In Mr. Thomas' final words, Grace saw a hint of the stern man she had witnessed up in the dining room. Yet, it was for Paden's protection. Perhaps, his attitude all along had been for Paden's sake. He had 'sentenced' his son, as Paden worded it, to a punishment below, but then paid Paden's debt with his own life. Only a loving father could do such a thing.

She turned with the child and moved towards the staircase, with Paden beside her.

"Paden," called Mr. Thomas' distant voice behind them.

She and Paden turned. Mr. Thomas said nothing. He stood upright, as tall as he could stand. His right arm was to his forehead in a noble salute to Paden.

Grace thought Paden's face was going to start melting again. Instead, he flashed his arm upwards into a return salute. It was a hasty 'goodbye', but it was beautiful.

"Let's move," said Grace, as they backed away.

Paden and Grace slugged through waist deep water, forcing their way towards the rear of Upper Deck. They had to shift their shoulders left, then right, then left, in a repeated fashion in order to negotiate the weight of the water on the legs. Little Anna clung to Paden, who now shared the burden of the extra load of responsibility. As they travelled down the deck, they heard faint cries for help.

"We can't stop," said Paden, as he hurried Grace who was trying to listen to the lost people. "The best we can do is shout. Wake them up."

Grace kept moving ahead of Paden and Anna, and started yelling. "Hello, down here! Wake up! The ship is sinking!"

"Hello!" chimed in Paden.

"Hello!" they both yelled in unison.

It was becoming difficult to hear whether there were any replies as water splashed down from the seams of closed doorways. Grace was afraid to open any doors, for fear of being overtaken by a wall of water, or knocked over by a dresser or, even worse—a dead body, now that the water had provided a means of travel. She started to notice obstacles that floated in her way: a dresser drawer, a child's doll, a wooden suitcase.

They managed to make their way past cabins and came to crew

facilities. They hadn't encountered any crewmembers, although they passed several other watertight door gears. The crew probably recognized that it was too late to do anything, but get up on deck to assist passengers attempting to flee.

"I hope the engineers are out," said Paden, as they approached an open door on the right.

The water was getting louder. Slapping. Like a strong current being channelled through a small rock space in a hillside. Passing a small hallway that housed some crew rooms marked 'Engineer', Grace discovered the source of the water noise. It was a porthole that had been completely compromised. A round force of water about the size of a tree stump ploughed through the hull with no chance of being forced back out. It reminded Grace of the little girl named Gracie, who told her parents that she didn't want to sleep by the porthole, for that was where the water would come in. *How wise that little child had been*, she thought, passing by the porthole.

"Paden. I'm scared," said Grace, realizing the water was quickly approaching her shoulders. "We have to move up. We have to go up now."

Paden nodded. "For once, we agree."

Although Grace could still touch the angled floor and wall with her feet, she began using her arms to pull the water behind her. She shivered every time the water splashed higher on her body, and had to keep moving so that her limbs wouldn't seize up.

A left turn. A staircase, leading back in the direction of the bow. Grace climbed the stairs with some difficulty, due to the slant to the ship. As they climbed the angled steps, there was some relief from the sting of the water as it became shallower, then disappeared. They appeared at the top of the steps and Grace ˙ noticed a door leading into a large open room. It was the Second Class Dining Saloon. It was dark and lifeless. Moving into the room, Grace observed that the water was collecting on the right side, the starboard side, and not on the rising port side.

"C'mon," said Paden, as he led Grace up the incline to the port side of the wide-open room, while dodging toppled chairs and a minefield of cutlery and dishes. At one point, Grace's wet feet slipped on the carpeted floor. Her ankle, still sore from the fall on the stairs, began to throb even more. Paden held onto Anna with one arm, and reached and grabbed Grace to help her up.

"I know it hurts," he said, sensing her pain and frustration, "but we can't stop, even for a minute."

At that moment, the ship lurched once again, as though shaken by an angry sea monster. The three fell to the slanting floor with such impact that Paden dropped Anna, sending her rolling down to the starboard side and under the pool of water. Grace caught a glimmer of a dark object forcing down upon her on the floor. She rolled to the side, but a part of something heavy attacked her forehead, followed by a song of short, twisted chords as the object toppled over in an inverted position. Clutching her open head wound with her hands, Grace looked. It was a piano.

"Save her!" yelled Grace, as she struggled, with her arms on the carpet, to regain control of her body's downward plunge.

Paden rolled his body in the direction of the fall, rather than attempting to stand and walk on an angle. He disappeared for a moment in the monstrous puddle of dark water, away from the faint glimmer of the emergency light. Grace crawled on her slippery, bloody hands and grabbed hold of the heavy piano leg for a little bit of security, although it had just clubbed her to the point of bleeding. She struggled to see Paden. Any objects more than a few feet away, dissipated into darkness. But, she knew he was working to save Anna, because she heard his voice reassuring the little girl.

"I've got ya'," he said. "Don't worry. I won't let anything happen to you."

"I'm scared," squeaked her tiny voice. Grace was relieved to see Paden emerge from the starboard tilt, standing with knees bent, and holding the hand of Anna. He reached Grace at the top of the incline, using tables and other debris for leverage. The incline had to be about thirty degrees by now, and getting worse.

It was a mere matter of minutes. They carefully manoeuvred through a doorway, to a passageway. Then, through a room. The pantry. It was the same area where the lift was located. Grace couldn't help but feel a momentary sadness for Eddie as she kicked pots, dishes, and mugs that had been strewn all around. But, there was so much more to feel sad about. *Will I make it out? Paden and the little girl? Where is Father?* These were the thoughts that tormented her now.

Paden pulled Grace by the arm to lead her through the darkened room to another door. She didn't really know where she was going, but was relieved to have a guide leading her through the shadows. They pushed through the door. And another door. A large room appeared and Grace knew it to be the First Class Dining Saloon. As she walked on the littered floor, she began wishing for her boots.

"Ouch!" she yelled, feeling something sharp under her feet. She looked down at the cold object and discovered it was a broken fragment of a dinner plate. Another step. "Ow!" A fork. She would have to focus her eyes carefully on where she stepped. She couldn't help but be amazed at how the table favours— carefully folded napkins, crafted centrepieces, accenting candles, and meticulously laid out cutlery—were spread in every direction. All the time afforded by many crew members—stripped away in minutes as though a tornado moved through the room.

They finally made it towards the door of the dining room

where voices of panic could be heard in the hall, at the foot of the grand staircase. A backlog of passengers was fighting its way through the passage. Some wore lifebelts. Others didn't. A crewman emerged holding several belts over his arm and called out, "Get these on, quickly!" He did not need to repeat himself as they were taken off his arm immediately and passed to passengers with fear on their faces.

Grace turned her attention to the staircase itself. The three were able to make it up to the Lower Promenade Deck after about a minute of negotiating the vertex of the stair and railing with their feet. As they reached the next portion of the staircase, leading to Upper Promenade Deck, the ship lurched some more. Grace and Paden had to bend down to grab the railing that was now almost completely at their feet. The gravity factor was worsening. Grace looked at what used to be the ceiling. The pear-shaped electric light fixtures, now dead, hung lifelessly from a once stronghold position.

She focused back on the task at hand—the stairs. Men and women were climbing on the spindle rails below, using them as a makeshift ladder. Some tried using the stairs, but slid sideways, banging into those on the rail. One man, dressed in a long white robe, attempted clinging to the left railing, now suspended in the air above him. He moved like a chimpanzee along tree limbs, his feet dangling above those glued to the railing below. When he arrived at the curve in the rail that continued upward to what was now their ceiling, he stopped abruptly, evidently out of muscle. He looked down with a gasp and plummeted on top of a woman who managed to reach the rounded corner on the other rail. The two toppled over the rail, careened the lower portion of the railing that curved to the deck below, and rolled off, onto the hard tiled floor.

The crewman who delivered lifebelts, a moment earlier,

lowered himself from his position at the bottom step, around the rail's fretwork, and let go, to fall near the two injured passengers. Other passengers watched, but dared not to let go of the rail.

Grace and Paden, with Anna tied to Paden's neck with her hands, slowly moved with the chain of passengers. The shadows of the frightened passengers in their matching lifebelts reminded Grace of spiders moving up a wall—a slow, but meticulous crawling of limbs.

Once rounding the lower curve of the rail, they were able to move easier out of the staircase by following the decline. Some of the passengers who were ahead of them, now walked and disappeared down the slightly flooded corridor towards the Music Room. Grace had a thought of going with them to check her room one last time to look for her father. But, as she noticed other passengers attempting to use the outer deck door below them, she noticed they fell into a pool of water up to their waists. The deck would not be a viable means of escape.

"Don't let go of the railing," said Paden, as he rounded the rail to become parallel with the starboard side. Grace grasped firmly, so as not to suffer the same fate of the man and woman on the stairs below.

"The deck entrance below is under water," she said looking down.

"We'll have to climb to the port side."

Grace looked up. *Portside. Up there!* she thought. *There's no way.* Paden continued along the rail, using muscles Grace didn't realize he had, given his skinny stature. She tried to move also, but felt the downward pull too overwhelming.

"Give me your hand," he said, now standing on the railing at the steps.

She reached up and he hoisted her to his position. Once safely secure on the rail, he jumped upwards and grabbed the other rail, much like the man downstairs did. Grace feared that he would loose his grip and bring them all down to the large puddle of water that was slowly, but surely, oozing its way through the outer deck door below. He was able to pull himself up, flinging his legs in the air and grabbing the rail with his feet. He rolled over the rail, immediately kneeled, then reached his arm down.

"Take 'old of the rail," he said to Anna, trying to get her off his back. At first, she resisted. "Please, Anna. It's the only way I can save Grace. Trust me. I won't leave you."

Slowly climbing off Paden's back, Anna took hold of the rail with both hands, as she knelt beside Paden. He reached down, stretching his arm as far as it would reach without compromising his legging. "Hurry," he said to Grace in a strained voice. "I can't hold much longer."

Grace felt an exchange of fingertips, but it wouldn't do. She would have to jump from the lower railing. As she did, she locked her left hand into Paden's right. He reinforced the grip with his other hand. She flailed for a moment suspended high above the starboard side doors that could barely be seen through the thickening window of water. He lifted her a few inches. Her other hand now gaining control, clutched his arm. He pulled back and up. She caught the rail, and mimicked Paden's legwork to help lift herself up on top.

Picking up Anna and putting her on his back, Paden stood and helped Grace stand. "The next part's going to be a trick, I'm afraid."

"What?" Grace gasped, as though her previous dangle of death was not enough. She looked up. The portside door to the outer deck above was at least eight or ten feet out of reach. They were at the end of their stair rails. Nothing else to pull themselves up with, or to use as leverage. Grace continued bending her neck upwards. She could hear scurried footsteps running along the deck above. Faint shoes echoed briefly as the owners came into contact with the wood door above them, shuddering the entry point each time, like several guns going off in sequence. She looked to the right of the rattling doorway. A stained-glass window allowed minimal grey light to shine through. Shadows passed by in sequence with each shudder of the door.

Grace looked down again. The deck doors were no longer visible. Any passengers on the starboard deck of the Upper Promenade were either under water, or struggling for any lifeboats that might have been launched.

"What are we going to do, Paden?" asked Grace, realizing they had to make a move now, or be trapped forever.

Paden spun around. To the left. Then, to the right. The answer was not up. That was obvious. It had to be across.

"Over here," he said, pointing across the deck from where they stood to the bow direction of the hallway. "See this hallway. We can jump across the staircase, into the hallway, and walk along the walls."

"Is there a door at the end of the hall?" asked Grace, fearing any thought of entering an even more confined space where she would have no chance of escaping.

"No," he said thinking. "But, we can get into one of the cabins…get into one and climb the furniture and crawl out a window."

Grace nodded. It was the best solution. Perhaps, the only solution. The main problem was the staircase. Although they stood firmly on the inverted rail, almost a ninety-degree inversion, they had to jump across the gap of the stairs where there was no rail.

"I'll go first," said Paden. "Hang on, Anna. Whatever you do, don't let go."

She issued a moan of panic, and tightened her noose around

Paden. He stood back a few steps. Looking down at the rail work, so that his feet wouldn't stumble between the frets, he skipped ahead, groaning as he made a giant plunge across. His arms hit the wall and he hung from the gap, with his right leg scrambling for a grip up above. He found footing and once again used his leg to assist in the pulling of his body, and Anna's to climb up to safety. Grace was amazed at how Paden seemed to have the technique learned so quickly.

"Your turn, Grace," he said reaching across to her as he and Anna stood on the walls of the corridor. With outstretched arm, Paden wiggled his hand to signal the expediency. Grace noticed Anna look down over the edge. Then at Grace. Anna took two steps back from the edge. Grace had felt a hint of confidence up until that point, when she was reminded of the consequence of missing the mark. It was a one-time deal.

She looked down at the rail, as her bare-feet did their best to feel her way across. Her eyes inadvertently shifted focus through the metal and wood spindles, where white, foamy waters danced many feet below. It would be a drop into oblivion.

"Grace," said Paden, reminding her that time was crucial.

She had to do it. Had to do it now. She hopped along the last remaining foothold pieces, and leaped across the stairway opening. She didn't get enough height and only hands caught the edge on the other side. With wet, numb fingers slipping down, she gasped.

Main staircase where many passengers fought an inverted climb

Chapter 12

Paden hit the wall floor and frantically grabbed Grace's arm. He had her, but she was slipping from his clutches. He dropped down and put his feet across to the side, pushing them hard against the tipped floor to pin himself in firmly. Using both hands, he pulled hard, using muscles all over his body.

As Grace rose, she saw his face. Although it was dark inside the ship, she could tell it was bloodshot. Now, assisting with the pulling by grabbing the ledge with her ankle, she climbed up and over Paden's body.

A small bump was felt, as a down and up 'hiccup' motion of the ship caused the three to stand and keep moving. Grace jumped up to the first cabin door above. The latch prevented its opening. Paden jumped in her place, trying to move the latch to the side. The door cracked open ever so slightly, but made a 'bang' on something above it.

"Must be furniture on top. A dresser or something," he said.

They walked along the wall, to the next cabin. Paden suggested to Grace that he hoist her up. He cupped his hands down low, and she stepped in. He was able to spring her high enough so that she could easily move the latch and push the door up. It was free of debris by the door. She pulled herself up with Paden's thrust from below.

"Anna," she said. Paden picked Anna up and threw her to Grace. Grace's body, now wrapped around a bunk bed, anchored her in place as she caught Anna, and moved her onto the wood side rail of the bunk. She reached down to grab Paden, who had already successfully jumped to take hold of the doorframe. He passed his hand to her, and she gave him a little extra assistance.

Once all three were in, they stood on the side of the bed. A dresser had been tipped over on the bed as well, and they were able to utilize it as a step to reach the sofa bed above, then the window. Grace was now thankful that the cabins on the ship were not all that big. If they were, the escape portal would be out of reach.

"I'll go out first. Pull you up," said Paden as he turned a latch and easily raised the windowpane upwards.

Paden didn't have to struggle too much to get up, as his head cleared the opening up to his underarms, and he allowed his arm strength to do the rest.

Grace lifted Anna up. Then herself. As she stood on the dresser and shot her head out of the hull, she was relieved to have the notion of being trapped inside the large tin can erased from mind. However, climbing out with the extra lift from Paden, she realized that she was being exposed to a whole new set of problematic circumstances. As they stood on the wall of the Upper Promenade Deck, with the floor's pine planks acting as a wall in front of them, Grace looked up and down the deck. There were passengers scurrying aimlessly across the deck wall. Some were young, some old. Both male and female. Donning lifebelts, or frantically seeking some. It was then, that Grace realized their next task.

"Paden, we—"

"Yes, I know," he interrupted. "We must find lifebelts. Then, a lifeboat."

They stood for a moment, dazed, as passengers flew past them in both directions. Grace became attuned to the surrounding noises. Human screams. They came from over the wall of pine. Over the railing. *They're clinging to the hull*, she thought. Other voices seemed more distant, and immediate concern was conveyed in their shorter, louder, higher-pitched wails.

"Here. Take this," came a voice. It was a crewman. He handed Grace a lifebelt. It appeared small, like a child's. She immediately bent down and wrapped it around Anna and tied it.

"We need to find a couple more," said Paden. "But, I don't think they're going to come as easy as that one."

Grace noticed others clinging to the same crewmen, who continued walking down the deck wall. "I'm sorry. I haven't anymore," he said.

"The lifeboats," said Paden, looking up, and back, towards the Boat Deck.

Grace followed his gaze, and realized that many of the lifeboats were not launched. The extreme list of the ship had made it impossible to liberate them. They rolled with the incline, towards starboard. Shadow people were seen further down the Boat Deck, strategically positioned on the rigging of the lifeboats, trying to free the lines.

"We have to get to one of those lifeboats," said Paden.

"But, it's no use," replied Grace. "They're trapped into the rigging."

Paden moved away from Grace and Anna, and climbed the wall to allow his body to access the rail of the Boat Deck, one deck up. Flinging himself over the rail, he immediately disappeared. Grace was feeling abandoned, wondering what to do. Several moments later, she saw his head reappear beside the steel hull of the leaning lifeboat. Down came a lifebelt. *He must have found it inside the lifeboat*, she thought. *Clever.* Grace was happy to have found such a resourceful person in Paden.

Sliding down the wall on his back, Paden returned to Grace's side. "Now, let's get up on the hull. See if we can spot a lifeboat in the water. These ones have no further use for us," he said pointing back to the Boat Deck.

Stepping back a few steps, Paden stopped, then ran forward. He jumped, kicked the inverted deck floor by raising his foot high, then grabbed the railing above. He was able to kick his leg over the railing and position himself on top. He looked around from his perch.

"What is it? Do you see anything?" asked Grace.

"Send her up," said Paden, nodding his head at Anna.

Grace picked up Anna. "Don't worry, Anna. Almost there," she said, lifting the child into the receiving arms of Paden.

"Now your turn," he said to Grace.

She repeated his earlier jump up the floor, and together with his help, hoisted herself over the railing. She turned away from the passengers that scrambled along the deck below and looked out on the hull as she stood. "Oh, dear!" she exclaimed. A myriad of figures clung to the deck, like insects on a log. They clung, positioning themselves. They lay. They crouched. They stood. Some walked. It was insane.

The three started walking. Carefully walking, towards the back of the ship's hull.

"It's 'ard to see the lifeboats," said Paden, because of the darkness. He was looking for handheld lights of the crewmen responsible for each lifeboat that had been launched. If any had been launched.

Crouching and shimmying their way past many passengers, who with bulged, still eyes, gazed down at the hull as they held on,

Paden and Grace made their way across the steel floor and looked out for signs of small vessels. At one point, Grace noticed that they were approaching a small shadow that moved, lower down on the hull, towards the water. It was too small to be a person. More like an animal.

"What is it?" she asked, looking ahead.

Before Paden could respond, she heard a noise. A voice. Coming from the small object. "Help! Someone help me!"

It was a head. Only a head. Poking through a porthole. A poor, unfortunate soul was still trapped in the giant metal prison, and would be dragged into the depths with her. The three moved towards the upper part of the hull above the man.

"It's too risky," said Paden, considering that they would have to descend the hull to rescue him.

Grace took Anna's hands and attached them to the railing and left her. She inched down several feet to get a better view.

"Please. Help me," pleaded the man, now turning towards the party of three above.

Grace focused her eyes on his shadowy face. She listened to his voice. A familiar feeling came over her. She turned to Paden. "Paden. I think it's the doctor."

He looked down at Grace. Grace looked at Paden. Paden had used the doctor for his selfish purposes earlier, and perhaps he felt some gesture or retribution was in order, for he inched his way down towards Grace. They moved together and reached the doctor's head.

The doctor reached his arms up. Paden tried to pull him up.

"Ow!" yelled the doctor. It wouldn't work. He couldn't fit through.

"Try one arm first," said Paden. The man slipped his right arm up, and kept his left shoulder down low. Paden pulled again. He struggled and out popped his left shoulder.

"You did it," exclaimed Grace. "Now pull underneath."
Paden reached underneath the doctor's arms, wedging himself behind the doctor's body, and lifted. The doctor cried in pain, as he rolled onto the hull.

"Thank you," he said, clutching his left shoulder. "Thank you."

"Let's get back to the railing," said Grace. They assisted the doctor up the hull, towards Anna.

"Let's head back towards the bow," said Paden.

"Go on without me," said Dr. Grant. "I just need a minute," he said, clutching his left shoulder, and hanging onto the railing with his right arm. Grace knew how he felt. Her ankle still throbbed from the stair fall, and she felt a large goose egg on her forehead from being hit by the flying piano.

Paden nodded to Dr. Grant and they left him. The three made their way back across the hull towards the bow.

Grace noticed another porthole beneath her feet. Though it was dark, she thought she saw a face looking up at her through the closed glass. She bent down to get a closer look. It appeared to be the face of a young woman, much like her. She stood straight up. "Paden. A young woman. We have to help her."

"Where?" he asked, approaching and following her stare downward. He reached down and looked. "Are you sure? I can't see anyone."

"She was..." spoke Grace, bending back down to the window. It appeared black. Nothing. She tried pulling on the glass. It wouldn't open, or even move the slightest. Did she see a young woman trapped below, now certain to pass on to death, or perhaps a reflected mirror image of her own face on the outer side of the window? They stood for a moment, but no face emerged. They would have to move on. As they approached the funnels,

Grace looked around at the hundreds of people, strung out on the port side.

"This is so incredibly horrible, Paden. We have to—"

Paden groaned sharply and fell backwards, landing beside Grace and grabbing her ankle to keep from falling off the hull to the depths, stories below. Grace fell to her feet and grabbed the railing to keep herself from being pulled down. She looked up. "What?" It was Steele. He knocked Paden down. *How did he—?*

"I'll be needing that lifebelt, Ms. Hathaway," said Steele. "Let's call it compensation for the eyes," he said, rubbing his eyes and cringing. He spread his feet apart, pulled up his shirtsleeves, and scowled like an angry grown-up bully.

Surely he wasn't serious, she thought. *After all this.* She stood and noticed that Steele was wrapping his right hand around a cord. The cord was attached to a bag. A mailbag. *Silver. He's still tied to the silver,* she thought in disdain. While he scared her, she was annoyed at how she had worked so hard to escape the inside of the ship, only to have her rescue become threatened by a selfish fool. "How far do you think you'll get with that stupid silver?" she yelled.

He lunged at her as she jumped back. She almost tripped on Anna, who crouched beneath, hands gripping the railing. Just shy of grabbing Grace, he fell forward. Tripped. Tripped by Paden. He jumped from his fallen position and grabbed Steele. The two wrestled in a lateral rolling movement on the hull for several seconds. Grace reached out to grab Paden so he wouldn't roll downwards and spill into the sea, but Steele kept emerging on top. Both exchanged punches, and elbows to the face. *This is madness,* she thought. *They're both going to end up falling. And there isn't time for this. We need to find a lifeboat, or we're all dead.* Grace kicked Steele in the face with her bare foot. He rolled off and Paden was able to break free. Paden immediately stood, and took a firm stance as Steele rushed him again.

"Watch out, Paden," yelled Grace.

Paden quickly sidestepped Steele, causing his former superior to fall again. Paden moved a few steps backwards, shuffling his feet away from Steele and towards the mailbag of silver.

What is he doing? Grace thought. "Forget the silver, Paden! We—"

Paden dragged the heavy canvas bag towards Steele. It was a wonder that Steele had been able to hoist it over the railing to the side of the hull. Steele rose to his feet and looked at Paden.

"You want the silver?" Paden taunted. "I hope you're willing to swim for it!" he shouted as he hoisted the burdensome bag knee-high in the air and looked down to the sea.

"Get away from my silver," barked Steele as he thrust his arms towards Paden's neck.

Paden ducked, allowing Steele to push behind him. Using both hands, Paden pulled Steele by the neck and pushed his head down. Rather than retaliate, Steele grabbed the bag. The cord of the bag wound around Steele's body as he spun around to grab Paden's throat again. Paden pushed him aside. Steele fell completely to his back and was dragged downward, headfirst, and face up, still clutching his bag of silver. Grace watched in horror as his body slid rapidly down the slippery hull, propelled by the weight of the silver that entangled him. He plunged into the tiny whitecaps that lashed many feet below.

The ship lurched again. "Grace, we can't stay here. This is getting us nowhere," said Paden, rejoining Grace and Anna at the railing.

"What can we do?"

"We can try going back on deck. Climb over to the starboard side. See there," he said pointing across the Boat Deck, in the water between the two funnels. From their vantage point where they stood, they could just barely view over the deck to see a couple of lifeboats quickly filling up with desperate passengers on the other side of the ship that was slanting down from them. Crewmen manned the boats, beacons of light in their hands, directing passengers. Individual voices couldn't be deciphered. Only massed vocal mayhem.

"Do you think we can make it in time?" she asked.

"It's our only chance. I'm guessing we only have a minute. Perhaps two."

As he said this, Grace guessed that it had only been about ten or twelve minutes since the ship had been struck, although it seemed much longer.

He jumped over the railing, hung for a second, then slipped down below to the deck. Grace passed Anna down, and then moved herself down. They climbed onto the top of a window frame, pulled themselves up to the edge of the Boat Deck, and climbed the rail. They didn't have to struggle to climb their way from here on, since the boats were a simple slide down the Boat Deck below.

"Let's go down here," said Paden. "We can use these to slow our descent," he said pointing at various metal casings. "That'll land us on the funnel. Then, we'll climb that skinny pole attached to the funnel, get a bit of height. Enough to land us in the water, next to that boat," he said gesturing at the lifeboat that seemed to be full of activity. "Then, I can worry about the next problem."

"Next problem?" she asked.

"Yes. I don't know 'ow to swim."

Grace couldn't believe it. Paden's parallel to Andrew was even closer than she had imagined. In any event, it seemed like a sound plan. There wasn't anytime for testing his theories in advance.

"Let's go," said Grace, holding Anna tightly on her lap as they slid down the deck a few feet. The splashing water had made the metal slippery, giving them an expedient slide to the various objects that they would use as large steps. Finally, their feet landed perfectly on the aft funnel. The residual warmth of the ship's steam could be felt all over Grace's body.

Paden helped lift Grace up the pole, and with Anna on her back, she was able to step on a few brackets that held the pole to the funnel. From her earlier soundings, Grace figured this slim structure to be the ship's whistle. Paden followed below her, and they successfully acquired enough diagonal height off the ship deck to land them in the water, almost directly beside the lifeboat. They would have to be careful not to hit the boat, or any scrambling bodies below.

"You 'ave to jump, now, Grace," said Paden.

She looked down. With Anna's legs and arms clutching Grace like a pole, Grace took one last look at Paden and let go of the pole. She dropped. Plunging below, the water felt colder than it had ever, now that she was fully submerged. Several feet below the surface, with Anna still attached, Grace found it difficult to swim up. She held her breath and hoped Anna would do the same.

A kick in the head. Several sets of legs blocked their surfacing. Grace had to use her arms and grab the flailing limbs and separate them. She surfaced. Anna began crying, in between gasps for air. Grace was relieved. They were both alive.

She pulled the water towards her to reach the boat. Welcome arms from a crewman reached down and grabbed Grace. Another pair of arms assisted, as the pair was hoisted together into the boat. Clutching one another as they fell to the floor, Grace and Anna were safe.

"Paden," said Grace, focusing away from herself. She looked up. He was still clinging to the pole. "What is he waiting for?" she asked herself.

Paden appeared to be trying to pull himself a little higher when a flash of white light appeared and a low bellowing sound was heard from within the vessel. The ship cried out. She would not slip away quietly. Angry fountains of water belched through the portholes into the air. The skylights on the Boat Deck shattered into millions of pieces into the air. Flying, flaming debris shot up and out from the vessel as floating passengers remained vulnerable targets. A taunting hissing sound followed, being accompanied by steam rising from the wreckage. "Must be the boilers," said the crewman on board the lifeboat, in response to the sound.

Grace looked up at the pole from which she and Anna had just fallen. Paden was gone. Disappeared. She looked around in the water. Light from emerging flames on the ship's Boat Deck cast a crimson glow on the faces of the unfortunate souls still in the water. Paden didn't seem to be among them.

She noticed another lifeboat moving away from below the tilting forward funnel. The crewmen were working hard at rowing away from the ship. It was then, that Grace realized the gravity of her own situation. The lifeboat that had taken her and Anna aboard was directly in the line of the aft funnel, should she come down.

"Move!" she yelled at her crewmen. "We have to move! Quickly," she said, standing and pointing up at the funnel above. It lurched. Down about a foot, then back up. Grace grabbed Anna in her arms and stood again.

"Sit down!" ordered a crewman.

"But, the—" she said, noticing the forward funnel in the distance was falling towards the other lifeboat.

With Anna in her arms, she jumped. A loud hollow 'wump' was heard underwater, as Grace struggled to surface with Anna again. She felt something hard hit the back of her legs. *It must be the lifeboat,* she thought. She swam and surfaced quickly enough to get air. Anna was still breathing. Looking back, she saw half of the mouth of the aft funnel, now filled with water, where her lifeboat used to be. No passengers or crew emerged from under the funnel. Had she not jumped that second or two earlier, she would have been clubbed by the giant smokestack.

However, she did not feel good about being back in the water. Now shivering again, her body felt like it was slowing down. She was too cold to do much more. She needed to get dry. Now!

She looked ahead to the other lifeboat near the sinking forward funnel. It was still there. Somehow, they had managed to escape its clobbering, if only by inches. The crewmen aboard were standing, using the oars to lift something. It was the Marconi wires. They had ensnared the small vessel. *If they're not successful,* she thought, *the Empress' snares will take the lifeboat down with her.* She continued swimming, with Anna on her back, towards the small vessel. It might get pulled down too, but it was her only hope.

She kicked and pulled the water behind her. She dropped her arms to rest them, but still kicked. Then, occasionally resting her legs, she used her arms. She felt some occasional relief, by lying on her side and swimming. If she didn't have Anna clinging to her, she might be able to try a few different strokes.

Nearing the last few strokes of the journey, she looked up and could see a flashlight aboard the lifeboat. It was moving around. She hoped it would point to her.

"Help…me," she stammered with a shallow, crackle of a voice.

The light pointed down in many directions, then into her eyes, where it remained. She had been found. Giving up on swimming, she just floated. Grace felt lighter as she realized Anna was not on her back. She panicked. *Where is she?* The thought of swimming back to find her in the darkness was torture. She didn't have anything left. She couldn't even conjure up the energy to propel herself completely to the boat, only feet away.

Suddenly, she felt herself moving, as though she had been given special powers. Only, it wasn't her.

"I've got ya'," spoke a voice into her ear. It wasn't until now, that she noticed an arm around her, coming up from under her left arm, although it was too cold to feel it on her numb body through the lifebelt. She was dragged a few feet in the water, and brought on side of the lifeboat. She looked into the face of her rescuer. It was a man in uniform. Ship's uniform. A crewman from the lifeboat had left the comfort and safety of his dry sanctuary and plunged 'neath the waters to try and pull her in.

"That's it, love. Give us your arms," spoke a voice from above. Grace cranked her neck out of the water. Through the glaring light, she could see arms reaching out for her. She returned their welcome by extending her arms, but they barely lifted above the waves. They were able to hoist her onto the side of the boat, the metal frame digging through her soaked nightdress and into her belly. She toppled, head first, into Lifeboat 1.

Shivering, and spent, she looked up at the pale faces of cold, frightened passengers. Like her, they were relieved to be afloat and out of immediate danger. But, Grace couldn't help but think of the likely fate of her father. Of Paden. And what of Anna?

*The Lower Promenade Deck, once a place of leisure,
most likely had become a slippery plunge for many into the water.*

Chapter 13

Using the icy legs of strangers as leverage, Grace pulled herself up to a sitting position. A woman passenger slid across the bench to allow Grace a seat. Grace spun around to search for the ship. The lifeboat crew, now having freed the boat from the wires, were rowing madly to distance the boat from the fallen ship.

The Empress, mortally wounded, let out one last wrenching cry, and disappeared from the horizon, into the depths of the St. Lawrence River. Immediately, Grace heard several gasps. A towering tidal wave was approaching their boat, from where the ship used to be. It was as though the ship was making one last attempt to kill her former occupants. The wave moved fast, but fortunately, the boat was turned in such a way that the wall of water hit her stern, and she rode with it for a moment. A short sigh of relief from all on board.

"Another one!" yelled a woman, looking in the direction of the missing vessel. A second wave drove at them, like the first. Crewmen rowed in fury.

"Don't let her come about!" one crewman insisted. Turning sideways at this point, would allow the water to topple the vessel, and it would suffer the same fate as her mother ship. A few more directions were communicated between the two crewmen aboard. The wave hit, and carried them away further. Grace kept careful watch that another wave was not on the dark horizon. After several anxious seconds, she allowed her body to relax and slouch her spine in her seat. She was relieved that the crewmen seemed efficient and seaworthy.

Looking beside her, Grace noticed a woman dressed in a fur coat, wearing a fancy hat, and appearing completely dry. Grace briefly looked herself over. Her nightclothes clung to her body, and the wet, shear fabric made it appear as though her legs were bare. Her ankle, although numb, felt larger than normal, and was difficult to bend. The lump on her head ceased bleeding, but felt extremely agonizing to touch. She would leave it alone.

She began to feel guilty for thinking of herself. Where was Anna? She looked across a few rows of passengers to see a passenger that sat lower than the others. She was shivering, not being comforted by anyone.

"Anna?" called Grace, now regaining some vocal chords.

The little girl turned. It was Anna. She conjured a smile. She turned completely, and lifted her leg over the bench to come towards Grace, crossing three rows of seats.

"Easy there, little one," spoke a crewman rowing.

Grace reached out to take Anna into her arms. She had forged a strong bond with this little child in only a short time frame. Cradling Anna, Grace tried to watch the activity in the water around her. Many voices were heard in the light breeze. Most were indiscernible. Too many at once.

Grace began looking over the edge of the lifeboat. They passed patches of floating debris such as wood riggings, pieces of furniture, and other unknown floating shadows. While it was dark, some of the ship's life buoys had freed themselves from the sinking ship. They approached one on the port side. Grace looked at the strange lime green light floating in the water that illumined objects around.

"There! Port side!" shouted the crewmen at the bow, pointing to a lifebelt floating alongside the nearest patch of glowing water. "Alive?" he asked.

Grace peeked over the edge of the left side. A body floated by. Arms extended freely. Mouth and eyes wide open. The green glow gave a sickly look to the face that was now flushed of life. She huddled Anna so that she wouldn't see the corpse. Looking around, she saw many silhouettes of other bodies, gently bobbing freely. Some, face first in the water.

Voices continued to jam the air. Some sounded angry. Two shadows appeared to be in conflict. Grace looked out. One man was trying to pull another person down. Or, at least, trying to stay afloat, at the expense of the other man, using him as a personal floatation device. The crewman behind Grace shone his flashlight on them briefly, but his beacon was re-directed behind the men to something shiny. It was a tub of some kind, being used by a woman who clung to the sides carefully, and kept a close watch at the water around her. The crewmen saw others in peril, but their boat was full. Grace was fortunate to have found hers in time.

After a few minutes, the voices in the night were beginning to quiet down.

"We've got to get to that other ship," spoke the crewman up front. He seemed to be the one in charge.

Grace thought for a moment. *Other ship? Another lifeboat?* Then it hit her. They had been struck by another ship. It must still be afloat. They could seek refuge from her. She looked into the dark horizon. A set of red and green lights was off in the distance. Her eyes followed them. They were becoming brighter.

A steady rowing speed allowed the lifeboat survivors to reach the offending vessel in a matter of minutes. Grace was not certain how many minutes. Just that time seemed to be moving quicker than before. Her whole concept of time had been thrown off by the traumatic events of the evening. But, she eventually made it to the Storstad. Grace noticed the ship's name emblazed on the crumpled bow in bold white lettering. *Seems she didn't suffer too much damage*, thought Grace resentfully.

Once Lifeboat 1 came alongside, the passengers were quickly hoisted up a ladder. On the deck of the Storstad, several crew officers and a woman greeted Grace and the other survivors.

"Here, take this," said the woman, offering a shawl to Grace. Grace wrapped herself in it. "Get inside," she continued. "Oh, you poor dears," she said, dispensing random nightgowns, sweaters, and scarves to the new passengers, some of them barely clothed. "I'm Mrs. Andersen. The captain's wife. Come with me."

The woman led Grace, Anna, and the other passengers inside the ship. They followed through a hallway, and several doors. The ship's layout and comfort was nothing in comparison to the Empress'. She was clearly a coal carrier, and not a people carrier.

The group shuffled into a large office that doubled as a bedroom. "This is my husband's cabin. Please rest here for now," said Mrs. Andersen.

Grace took Anna, and propped her on a sofa and leaned her head against a wall. She collapsed beside her. Grace's body was beginning to shiver at a slower rate. She felt her heartbeat slow, and she was able to move the rising and falling of her chest in sync with that of Anna.

Inside the room, passengers and crewmen collapsed on chairs, the floor, and tables covered in charts and maps. Grace didn't move for the first few minutes, until she could regenerate.

Another load of souls was ushered into the room. They took

up remaining spaces and lay shivering, still trying to acclimatize to their new surroundings.

"We better start sending them below, in the engine room, and near the boilers," spoke Mrs. Andersen. A crewman nodded to her, and they both exited together.

At this time, Grace mustered enough energy to look around the room and survey her fellow occupants. Many of them were not properly clothed. Some wore only their undergarments, nightclothes, or corsets. Some wore makeshift clothing supplied by the captain's wife. Drapes. Potato sacks with holes cut out for legs. Men, wearing women's clothing. One man wore only a scarf around his midsection.

Mrs. Andersen returned with some bottles. Grace read the word 'whisky' on one of them. "Here," said Mrs. Andersen, gesturing around the room. "Take sips of these and pass them on. It'll warm you up, some."

Grace watched as the bottles were passed around. She was dumbfounded as she observed cultured ladies and gentlemen swigging out of the shared bottles. When a bottle came around to her, she was going to pass it by, but then took hold of it. Holding out her hand, she poured some alcohol and rubbed it on her head wound. It stung harshly, but made her more alert.

"Can I look at that?" asked a man.

Grace looked across the room at a man staring at her open head wound. Grace couldn't believe her eyes. It was Dr. Grant. The man she and Paden had rescued from the porthole. She was quite relieved he got out.

"I think it will be fine," she replied. She wanted to share with him about their earlier meeting, but then heard other voices.

"You a doctor?"

"Doctor, please help me."

"And me too, doctor."

She would have to wait. Dr. Grant assumed his expected role, assisting various passengers with their wounds. He wound and tied items of clothing around various cuts and assessed many for broken bones. All the time, Grace noticed him cradling his wounded shoulder, obvious trauma from the porthole deliverance. Yet, he never said a word to anyone about it. *What a gracious man*, she thought.

Grace began to speak to Anna. "Are you feeling better?" she asked. It was a stupid question. How can she feel 'better' after losing her parents, and almost dying several times, in several different ways?

Anna simply nodded, and flashed a childlike smile.

Grace felt that she could slip into sleep instantly.

She shook. Startled. Grace, with Anna in her arms, guessed that she herself had been asleep for an hour or two. Her eyes found time on the wall. It was 4:18.

Grace woke because of a commotion across the room. The doctor was speaking with a man whose face was buried into his hands.

"Captain Kendall?" spoke the astonished doctor in a loud voice.

"Leave me alone," said the captain in an obvious state of brokenness. "They should have let me drown with the others."

"Don't be foolish," exhorted the doctor.

"The man sunk my ship," continued the captain.

Grace lost much of the remaining conversation as the doctor tended to the captain and assisted him in lying down. The captain appeared to be exhausted, but managed to speak as he moved.

"We went back out. Tried to get them. Many as we could find. So many lost." He explained in few words how he was pulled into a lifeboat, and came to the Storstad. He ordered the lifeboats out into the waters again to look for more survivors. He himself commanded one. He mentioned other ship names—the Lady Evelyn, and the Eureka, that were dispatched to rescue survivors. Grace remembered the Lady Evelyn as the ship that received the last dispatch of mail, and almost received an unexpected dispatch of silver and a defiant passenger with a used revolver.

How Grace wanted to ask the captain many questions. *What happened on the bridge? Why did the ship collide with another? How did you survive, when so many others were dying?* One thing was certain. He would have many questions to answer when he returned back to shore.

She struggled to listen to more of the conversation. Bits about miscommunication, uncertainty, were relayed. Ships changing directions to avoid a collision. Then, she heard something that jolted her and caused her to sit upright from her comfortable slouch on the sofa.

The doctor, upon listening to the captain's account of various events, replied, "Perhaps, if you and Captain Andersen had done nothing—not acted in any way—then our two ships may have passed by each other without so much as a whistle being blown."

Grace thought about this notion. She had been on the Boat Deck when the whistles blew. The ship had stopped. *Where would I be—where would we all be right now if the two captains had ignored each other and didn't attempt to reposition themselves in the water? If Captain Kendall hadn't stopped the ship, putting us dead in the water! If Captain Andersen had stayed on course!* Fog shrouded their judgment and caused disaster.

Grace realized that she was sufficiently rested and warmed to look after her next priority. Find out the plight of her father, and her new friend, Paden. She lay Anna down on the sofa in the space that she had previously occupied, being careful not to wake her. She wrapped herself in a blanket that lay by the door and exited the captain's office.

Grace found her way out on deck. The cool night breeze seemed refreshing now that there was certainty that it would do no harm to her. She watched as scattered distraught passengers huddled nervously on deck. Some of them were still seeking solace inside, but others had the same notion on their minds as Grace. Find their loved ones. She felt it difficult to look as husbands, wives, mothers, and fathers, wept bitterly. She didn't see any children, and could only hope that they were inside, or on the Lady Evelyn or Eureka.

She limped slowly along the low, long, straight deck, scanning the shadowy faces and figures she passed. She had to look twice at some of them to see if she recognized her father or Paden. Many of these people were obviously dishevelled and looked different from before. Opened wounds, bloody faces, burnt skin, and lack of proper clothing gave evidence to their unusual appearance as the result of an unthinkable event.

As she moved without success of her deepest desire, Grace was running out of deck, and approaching the front of the bow. If she didn't find her father very soon, the chances would be remote. The bow came into clarity as she approached, being as it was near morning light. Several ship officers stood at the Storstad's front, keeping people from moving too close, meanwhile assessing the hull damage. Grace could see the mangled metal that had intruded into her life and the lives of so many others, cutting wounds that would bleed forever. She was relieved to be safe on board her deck, but hated her for what she had done. The Empress sat there quietly and didn't deserve to be carved open like a fish from a swift fisherman's blade.

Turning around to go back down deck, Grace was startled by a figure, one step behind her, staring at her with wide eyes and red and black streaks down his face. She should think that he was a monster, but recognized his eyes.

"Grace? It is you! You're alive!"

"Father? Father!" She opened her blanket and clothed the both of them in it as they embraced. "I thought you were...you disappeared below and..." She couldn't explain herself as she was overtaken with sobs in her throat.

"Grace. This is a miracle. I thought I'd lost you." He embraced her some more. "I really didn't think I would see you again. I can't believe I almost..." He stopped and looked at her forehead. She held her hand to her wound in response. "What has happened to you Grace?" he asked as he assisted her limping body to a resting position on a metal container.

In her best recollection, she told of her encounter below with Paden and Anna. How Anna's father had entrusted his daughter with Grace and how Paden's father had sacrificed himself. She spoke of their narrow escape from within the hull of the ship, to join the party above on the outer hull, then to struggle in the water. She considered telling him about Crall and the plot to steal the silver, but decided it was not important. At least, not at this time.

"How did I let you go?" he asked. "You should have been by my side."

Grace didn't know how to respond to this. Then, she was curious. "What happened to you, Father?"

Her father told how he was unable to sleep. Grace was surprised to hear that he had difficulty sleeping, being troubled by the events of change that were taking place in their lives.

"As I lay in bed," he said, "I felt as though I was missing something. That something was you. I leaped from my bed, pulled open the curtain to your bed and saw you gone. As I scrambled to pull on some clothes, I felt that the ship had stopped. I peered out the window to see a ship…this ship," he said pointing downward to the floor, "coming directly for us. When she collided with us, I ran to wake Harriet, then began searching for you."

"You went below?" asked Grace.

"Yes. I searched as long as I could. The lights went out. The water poured in. I didn't know where I was going. I waded through the cold water infiltrating the decks, until it rose above my head. Bending my neck to kiss the ceiling for air, I was pulled in a current. Someone grabbed me. I was hauled up to the next deck through a stairwell, above the water line. It was a crewman. He insisted I take a lifebelt and follow him upstairs to safety. I didn't want to go, and would have stayed below deck to the very end until I could find you. But, I went with him, for one reason alone."

"What was that?" asked Grace.

"I thought, if Grace made it out—if she is safe, then I must get out too. For her sake. I would have risked death to save you, but I didn't want you to face death again. You have experienced more of your fair share of that lately."

Her father spoke words of comfort to her. Grace couldn't believe how he went to the bowels of the ship to save her. How he now regretted the possibility of losing her. It was something she hadn't experienced in awhile. She reached out to him in empathy.

"And poor Harriet," she said, assuming the worst, because of her noticeable absence.

"Harriet?" said her father. "Harriet is alive. She is here on the Storstad. She is resting just over…" He pointed, but could not see her to complete his sentence.

Grace was stunned. She assumed that since she wasn't by his side guiding his every move, she had been taken to the depths below. Grace didn't know how to feel. Certainly, she wouldn't wish a grave upon anyone. She would have to be an awful person to contemplate that. However, she had found comfort in the thought that she had her father back. Her turmoil would continue. Her father's sympathy for her would not be enough to combat the snares of this woman.

"She made it!" sounded a voice. Grace and her father turned. It was Harriet, with Winifred a few steps behind. "I can't believe you got out, after such a reckless descent below deck. A selfish act which almost cost your father his life."

As Harriet approached Grace's face in the early morning darkness, Grace could not believe that Harriet looked completely dry. She wore her nightclothes, covered by a robe, topped off with her elegant hat with feathers. She obviously stepped easily into a lifeboat without worry.

"If this is the kind of behaviour I can expect from this child," she continued scolding, first Grace, then her father, "then I shall say that boarding school is looking more and more attractive by the minute."

"Boarding school?" said Grace alarmed. *First, he replaces Mother, and now he gets rid of me?* she thought.

"Harriet, dear. I don't think you should be—" said her father, but was cut off by Harriet.

"That's just it, Jeremiah. You don't think. You didn't think of anyone but yourself when you abandoned me in peril on the Upper Promenade and went chasing this foolish girl. Did you forget your place?"

Grace stood with her mouth opened and couldn't speak. It was the same immobilizing feeling she had encountered in the water when she had spent all her energy and was ready to give up.

She looked to her father. He turned away from Harriet and looked over the ship's rail to the surrounding silhouettes of

Canadian hills that were engulfing the waters they sailed. He appeared to be thinking. Then, he turned to Harriet and spoke.

"Yes. Perhaps I have forgotten my place. My place is here, with my daughter. Nothing, and certainly no one will come between that, my dear."

Grace couldn't believe her ears. Had she heard it wrong in the wind? She felt the same silencing surprise as when she learned moments earlier, that Harriet was still alive.

"What are you saying?" asked Harriet, with no restraint on her tongue. "You aren't coming to England?"

He nodded.

"Our marriage?"

He shook his head.

"How dare you! Do you know how much time has gone into our wedding? Do you have any inclination as to the trouble you are causing? You have disgraced me! My family has the power to—"

"Your family has no power over me," he said. Turning his back on her, he took Grace by the arm and moved away from her. Embellished sobs were heard in the background.

Her father's defence of her elated Grace. Of his dismissal of Harriet. He burned his bridge to a life with her, with his usual swift manner.

"Grace, my love," he said as they moved to an empty rail, away from other rescued passengers and crew. "I have something for you."

"Something for me?"

"Yes. Well, actually, I have two things for you." He reached into his right jacket pocket. "Firstly, I have this." He pulled out an object on a long thin chain.

"Is that…is that my—"

"Your necklace. With your mother's picture. I know you

wanted to keep it safely stowed in the ship's safe. I considered your request, but then felt that the safest place for your mother was here," he said, tapping his hand to his inside jacket pocket above his heart.

"I thought I had lost it forever," she spoke in earnest, lifting her hair off her shoulders and allowing her father to connect the latch behind her neck, to hold the cherished item firmly in place. Grace smiled, but remembered. "And the second thing?"

"Well," said her father, clearing his throat and reaching back into the same jacket pocket. "I'm really surprised it survived the dumping into the river."

He pulled out a folded piece of writing paper. Carefully unfolding its soaked layers, he revealed a handwritten note. She immediately recognized the handwriting. It was her mother's. Grace had always admired her colourful scribing. He passed it to her. They both instinctively moved several feet in the direction of a deck lamp to allow the reading.

My dearest Grace,

I deeply regret having to leave you. The doctor says I haven't much time left. Months. Maybe weeks. Time can be so unpredictable in such matters. In any event, I wanted you to know that I have treasured the time that I have spent on this earth with you.

Some years ago, your father and I wanted to have a child so eagerly, but were unable to, for some unknown reason. The doctors couldn't give us definite answers as to why. The only definite was that we would never have a child. Then, one warm summer's day, we discovered that you were in our future. We were taken away with delight, as we most certainly gave up any hope of a child. We named you 'Grace', since you were a blessing to us.

Because you are such a special child who deserves continued blessing, I have suggested to your father, that he acquaint himself with a cousin of mine in England, who knows of a man whose daughter wishes to wed. A marriage to this woman would certainly do no harm to anyone seeking security of stature and future wellness. I believe it is in your best interests, as well as those of your father, that he seek to nurture a relationship with this family, in order to give you continued life and happiness in a world that, unfortunately, will be void of me. For these past years, I have worked among the less fortunate. This has caused a strain to our family's finances. I must say with true sincerity, that I would see difficulty in resigning my family to be among the less fortunate that I have served.

I have asked your father to give you this note on the day of a future wedding, should this plan employ. I trust that you will not feel bitter toward Father, myself, or his new bride. I ask that you move on, and do not allow yourself to be weighed down with anxiety or guilt.

It is with a heavy heart that I compose this letter. I now entrust you into this world. May it find a haven for Grace.

Most lovingly,

Mother.

Grace was tight-lipped. She needed to process the information for a moment, before giving a response to her father. She was uncertain how to feel. The union with Harriet—it was all her mother's plan—not her father's. She had blamed him for replacing her mother so quickly. 'A swift action is the best action,' he would always say. She boarded the Empress with so much resentment for her father's reckless abandonment of her that she did not realize his sacrifice for her all along. Only her own needs. Her own entitlement. She believed him to be the selfish one.

Grace thought back on her Wilkshire Mansion murder novel, and the number one rule of mysteries. *The culprit is always the person that is least likely to have done it.* She forgot that rule when she erred in trusting Steele. And now, once again, she erred in thinking that she couldn't possibly be in the wrong. In actual fact, she had been the culprit all along. The guilty one. She had dwelt too much on her innocence, all the while, her father was the one who lived sacrifice.

"Father," she spoke. "Do you love her? Harriet, I mean?"

He hesitated, suggesting an answer in the delay. "Love. I thought I did...would...in time. But, perhaps the time would never come for that."

"But, you were willing to sacrifice true happiness for me? Why did you go along with Mother's plan?"

"You know me, Grace. I am a man of action. Her plan seemed an expedient fix to a problem I knew not how to solve."

Grace recollected her time in Captain Andersen's office. "Father. Shortly after being brought aboard this ship, I shared the same company as the doctor and the captain of the Empress."

"Captain Kendall? He's alive?" questioned her father with a rising gaze into Grace's eyes.

"Yes. I heard the captain talking to the doctor about the collision of the ships. The doctor made an interesting statement."

Her father tilted his head in curiosity.

"Upon hearing the captain's account of the events leading up to the disaster, he said that perhaps the collision would have been avoided altogether, if neither captain hadn't acted at all—hadn't changed course, or stopped. If they hadn't jumped to action, you and I would be sleeping quietly in our own cabin aboard the Empress right at this instant."

"I see," said her father, understanding the relevance of her account to their situation. "Then, perhaps sometimes, the best course of action is no action at all."

Grace nodded.

He continued. "I guess there are just some things you can't work for. You just have to accept, Grace."

She felt his arm wrap around her shoulder over her blanket. For the first time in a while, Grace felt at peace with her father. She believed that now, they would both together, return to Canada, her home, and face the unknown. The immediate unknown, especially, would be the most challenging. She needed to find out whether she would celebrate or mourn her new friend, Paden.

Crumpled bow of the Storstad

Chapter 14

Grace stood reverently with her head slightly bowed. Sixteen bodies lay neatly in their caskets, in rows, each parallel and carefully spaced apart from one another. Banners draped the top of the caskets—purple, white, and black. She stood with the crowd of hundreds that had formed the procession of horses and carriages, starting near Toronto's Massey Hall theatre on Shuter Street, and up Yonge Street to Mount Pleasant Cemetery. Most of the family and friends wore black. Many of them wore their Salvation Army uniforms, given this was a funeral honouring sixteen of the many Salvationists on the Empress. They would forever remember this day, June 6, 1914, as the day they sang 'Til we meet again', and meant it.

As she stood with the crowd at the cemetery in a 'V' formation around the bodies as they lay in their caskets on the gentle sloping of the grass, Grace paused to think about things. The funeral she attended at the Mutual Street Arena. The lovely children's choir, about one hundred voices singing while positioned in a giant, hollowed cross on the arena floor, facing the rows of sixteen caskets.

The many blank faces of the one hundred thousand people

lining the street, watching and weeping. Grace walked among the mourners, about a third of the way from the front. The procession began with many flags, and was followed by a carriage containing a myriad of flowers. Four horse-drawn lorries, each carrying four caskets laden with flowers, also followed. The four horses pulling each lorry were draped in grey, and were accompanied by walking pallbearers, apparently family members of the deceased. Beside the children's caskets, walked a number of young children. Following the children, walked Grace and a number of other survivors who lived or stayed near Toronto. More bands followed behind. Grace was impressed with how the city stood still for this event. Shops closed. Streets closed. People standing still and sombre.

There were different degrees of mourning. While she didn't know the dead personally, she had engaged them on board the ship, just over a week earlier. She had walked where they had walked. She had seen the tragedy they had seen. She felt that she had earned a place among them. Others, simply stood as curious bystanders, witnessing the unprecedented event.

It was difficult to focus on the words being spoken on the cemetery lawn. Her mind drifted back to Quebec. When the Storstad pulled into the pier at Rimouski, how she desperately wanted to see Paden standing on the dock, waving his uniform cap that so awkwardly fit. Instead, she saw mounds of bodies, overlapping and smothering one another in a coal shed at the end of the wharf. Her father begged her not to go there. But, she had to see for herself. It was madness. Husbands and wives, mothers and fathers, grandparents and children, all searching for their loved ones that day as they were unloaded from the Eureka and the Lady Evelyn. Grace had watched Dr. Grant take charge of the unloading of the dead from the Storstad, and knew that Paden wasn't among their dead.

Sadness and joy were the order of the day when people discovered the fortunate or tragic news of their families. In some cases, Grace noticed both. While walking the pier, she saw a woman walking lifelessly towards the end of the line of bodies. Hope had disappeared from her face, when a voice was heard from behind Grace.

"Momma!" cried the child. "Momma!"

Grace turned to see the young girl, maybe a six or seven-year-old, running towards the awaiting arms of her mother.

Another woman loudly wept on the ground, clutching a man's body by his nightshirt. "Dear Harry," she moaned, rocking back and forth in sitting position. "My dear, Harry." She stopped rocking. She picked up the lifeless arm. "That's not your wedding ring." She scrambled to her feet and began surveying the other bodies.

Grace had discovered through reports that mistaken identity had played a cruel trick on many. Some parents mistakenly claimed bodies of children that were not their own. Others were told that their loved ones had survived, but didn't, and vice versa. She was shocked to learn that initial reports were given to The Salvation Army that all the Empress passengers and crew had survived. With such mind-wrenching turmoil, it seemed that the Empress tragedy was not confined to the water. Like the wave that immediately followed the Empress' sinking, the wave of fear continued to roll over her passengers.

Paden was still a mystery. In all the published lists of passengers and crew that were lost, Grace could not find Paden's name. She found a Thomas. It was Assistant Chief Steward Thomas. Paden's father. She was saddened to read his name on a list posted outside of Toronto's Canadian Pacific Railway office, but was not surprised, knowing she and Paden were most likely the last ones to see him alive.

With head still bowed, Grace closed her eyes on cue of the gentleman speaker, someone named Commissioner McKie, who signalled a moment's silence. The cemetery streamed with people standing shoulder to shoulder around the caskets, while others peeked over the fence in the background, and a multitude of people waited outside the tall stone gates that were a short walk back to the street. Yet, all was silent.

Her mind continued pondering this surreal moment. How did she happen to be here? She had never attended or imagined an event like this? A short number of days ago, she was no one. She blended in with the crowd of passengers. No one cared about her, or knew she existed, or was aware of where she was going. By now, published lists of survivors had travelled all around the world and people were being awakened to the new reality. Strangers in different countries would read her name outside the CPR offices, or in the local newspapers. It was as though there was a giant earthquake, with the Empress at the centre, and multiple shocks, powerfully spread out in every direction, to multiple countries. It was unusual. But, then again, all the events that she had lived in the past number of days were not normal. An orderly world had flipped upside down.

Even the train ride home to Toronto was like a terrible dream. Unlike the ride to Quebec City. Now, people weren't joyful, anticipating the journey ahead. People of varying classes and walks of life accompanied one another and, in some cases, assisted one another. Those who wore new outfits for the journey across the Atlantic, now wore tattered, or embarrassingly inappropriate clothing. Humility was the due course now.

Money took on a new position in this new reality. There were no tickets to be collected on this rail ride. Passengers were simply loaded freely without question. Grace had read a newspaper report that the Empress' senior Marconi operator, Ronald Ferguson, travelling with survivors aboard the Lady Evelyn, had been requesting payment from survivors wanting to send messages to their relatives. After a short-lived cry of opposition, Ferguson began sending transmissions without payment. Grace was also surprised to hear passengers on the train complaining about losing their wallets, and one woman near her spoke about pursuing a lawsuit against the Canadian Pacific Railway for damages and losses to her family, and hoped to receive a substantial payment.

At this, a man stood. "How can you?" he asked with conviction in his eyes. "How can you think of such a thing at a time like this? I would part with all that I have, just to see my Nora alive." He sat down.

Grace stared at the floor as the train car went silent, hearing only the shudder of the iron wheels on the track below as the passengers gently swayed from side to side.

One of the train cars, called the Madawaska, a sleeping car, had been converted to a makeshift hospital. A place designed for rest, now was administering a different type of comfort. Grace had peeked in through the doorway of the car, but did not want to get in the way of those wandering in and out as they tended to the wounded.

And the train didn't slip quietly into Toronto, but was greeted by an eager crowd of thousands, including relatives, reporters, rail officials, and police. It had been a frightening ordeal with the mass of anxious greeters, pushing to get at Grace and the other survivors. It was a stark contrast to the cheerful send-off that took place in Quebec City. No music. No pleasant waving. Simply noise and confusion.

The silence continued for a moment, when Grace noticed people putting their caps back on their heads, as she raised her head once again. The coffins, smartly dressed, would soon be lowered into the ground.

Following the ceremony, Grace observed some mourners lingering near the graves, hugging and clinging to loved ones. Others said their farewells, and moved on with conviction that they would have to adapt to a new life without them.

Grace backed away from the site, and regrouped with her father and her Aunt Nona across the small roadway in the cemetery. Having her aunt live nearby made it easier for her and her father to stay around the city during this time. *Perhaps, this would become our permanent home,* she wondered.

Grace looked at Anna, holding her aunt's hand, and gazed across the path at the lingering mourners. She wondered what Anna was thinking. Did she fully comprehend that she would never see her parents again? Grace's father had found their names on a posted list as having perished. Joel and Sylvia Anderson. Anna's name was also posted as having survived, in the unlikely event that her parents had survived and were looking for her, or that perhaps, a relative would identify her. That never happened. Instead, Grace's father turned his attention into inquiring about his sister's adoption of little Anna.

"Shall we go?" tendered Grace's father in a caring voice.

"Yes, I suppose," said Grace. She took one last look at the gravesite. She turned to the direction of the gate and stepped onto the path. As she slowly walked with others, now starting to leave, she noticed a man walking against the flow of people, filtering towards her. But, he wasn't quite fully a man. It was a young man. He was tall and slender, with a youthful look. He swam in his black suit that looked borrowed from a wider person. His face was scarred, and he walked with a limp.

As he moved towards her, his face surfacing out of the shade of a tree, he spoke. "It is good to see ya', Grace."

"Paden!" she exclaimed. She couldn't believe it. She had given up hope of seeing him again. Grace rushed to him and the two embraced in a hug, until Paden pulled away in discomfort.

"Sorry. Me back is still suffering a bit. But, I'm alive."

Grace smiled for the first time since the disaster.

"Looks like you've had it rough, too," he said looking at Grace's head and unstable leg as she had one ankle raised slightly off the ground. He shook Grace's father's hand. "Mr. Hathaway. Glad to see you made it out, too."

Her father smiled and nodded.

Paden turned to Anna. "And you! Do you remember me?"

The girl released Nona's hand and plunged towards Paden and wrapped her arms around him, shutting her eyes as tight as she could.

"Ah, that's all right," he said welcoming her. Slowly bending down with obvious back pain, he knelt at her eye level. "You were a brave little girl. You were." Looking up to the others, he asked, "Parents?"

Both Grace and her father shook their heads.

He turned back down to Anna. "And now, we need you to be brave some more. Can you do that for me?" he asked.

She nodded in a trusting, childlike fashion.

As he stood, Paden put his arm around Anna, and told his account of his rescue, for Grace and the others were very eager to hear. "The last time I saw you, Grace, I was hanging from the pole, just above the lifeboats."

Grace nodded to affirm.

"Next thing I knows, a huge explosion from inside. I'm thrown off, into the water. I pull upwards, but there's legs everywhere above me in the water, kickin', flailin'. I finally get my 'ead above water and struggle to stay afloat. I'm grabbin' at people, beggin' for help. But, the lifebelts. They only support one person. I didn't want to take anyone down with me."

"Then, what did you do?" asked Grace curiously.

"It's not so much what I did. It's what was done for me. Outta' nowhere, a man comes and shoves a lifebelt in me face. 'Put this on,' he says insistently. By now, I'm eager to oblige and he 'elps me get it wrapped and tied around me. I was thankful, because in the cold water, I didn't know how much longer I could 'old out."

"You were so fortunate that someone had an extra," interjected Grace's father.

"Well, that's the thing. I quickly noticed the man struggling to stay afloat. I grabbed him, but he kept sinking the both of us. You see. He didn't give me an extra lifebelt. He gave his one and only lifebelt, so that I might live. And when it wouldn't support the both of us, he swam away from me so that I could stay afloat."

"That is incredible," said Grace. "He sacrificed himself for you."

"That's only the half of it. Before he swam away, he looked me in the eyes with intent. 'Now, you are saved', he said. I noticed a short beard on the elderly man. I looked into his eyes. I remembered him. It was him. It was the man. The Salvationist that I met at the start of the voyage when we were up on deck. I was stern and rude with him. Told him I didn't need savin'. Turns out, he was right. And he died for me."

Grace was amazed at Paden's reaction. The crisis had changed him. He was not the arrogant young man. He was now a sober, appreciative grown man.

"And that is why I am leaving for England immediately."

"You're going back to England?" asked Grace. She had been hoping that he might stay in Canada, as a newfound friend. But, he would have other concerns. "I guess your mother will be anxious to see you again."

"Most certainly. But, that is not the only reason. The recent events have caused me to give thought to my life."

Grace was taken back at Paden's words, but was delighted to listen to his mature tone.

"I have spent the last number of years on myself. Seeking what's best for me. I stole and cheated. All the while, I justified it by saying to myself, 'I'll pay it back someday. Someday, when the time comes and I 'ave enough money, and don't need to take from others.' Unfortunately, it took the sinkin' of a ship for me to realize that my time was runnin' out. All the lousy things I had done. There wouldn't be time to pay them back, and soon I'd be dead." Looking her in the eyes. "Grace," he said, "if you hadn't pulled me outta' the ship when I went down below, you know, by remindin' me of my sister's death, then I'd probably 'ave stayed down there. My body would be in the ship now. I would be spending my eternity below."

He turned to her father. "Now that I have been saved by Grace, I must respond. I am going back to England to enlist in the army. There have been murmurs of a great war coming."

Grace's excitement about seeing Paden alive and well began slipping into worry. *Does he know what he's getting into? He could be killed.* However, she knew him well enough to know that changing his mind would be a difficult thing. That, and her feeling inspired to see this new man caused her not to protest too much.

"Are you sure about this?"

He nodded. "I'm getting the CPR to arrange passage on another ship. As soon as the confusion settles."

"What will you do in the meantime? Where will you stay?" she asked.

"Arrangements have been made from the CPR office."

The conversation continued for a short time, until Grace returned with her family and Anna, to her Aunt Nona's house. Grace's father convinced Paden to come and stay in his sister's house for the duration of his stay, so that he could be with friends.

Paden gladly obliged the family, and enjoyed their company for about a week, until his ship was due to go out.

Grace would never forget the sight of this young man, having said a final 'goodbye', turning and walking towards the double doors of the Toronto train station to catch his train. He would begin his journey of a new life. He kept to the concrete walkway that stood alone in the centre of a large muddy patch. All other ground was sinking sand. The street area itself, showed signs of devastation and rebirth, following the fire that swept away the old Union Station in 1904, and the plans of rebuilding, later this year.

The time she spent with Paden since meeting him, just over two weeks ago, seemed rather short. She knew she would probably never see him again, but she would not forget him. She had bonded with him, and had grown with him. He had inspired her with his survival story, and his desire to serve others.

She learned that there were two ways of looking at the Empress disaster—a curse, or a blessing. It all depended on whom you talked to. For her, she knew not why she had survived, above others. She certainly didn't feel as though she had merited salvation. Yet for some reason, she was saved. She could look at the sinking, like so many others, as a terrible thing, like the Crippen Curse. She could seek restitution from the CPR officials. She could spend the rest of her days feeling sorry for herself, as others might be prone to do. But, she had a sense that the tragedy had brought wholeness. Leaving Quebec City harbour, she never considered the possibility that she would return home to Canada. Now, she was back with her father and aunt. Her aunt, having never recovered from the loss of her son, now had a little child in the house to care for, once again. Anna, an orphan, would again, have the warmth of a loving upbringing. Somehow, amidst tragedy, there seemed to be hope.

Grace knew that she, and others who faced death up close,

who witnessed unimaginable things, who thought they would most certainly die, had been freed from a lie—that time lasts forever. Paden had given her the idea. It was one important truth that bore in her brain. His notion of time. He spoke of not having enough of it. As she began to think about her own circumstances, she realized that her own concept of time had evolved. She used to believe that time was constant—that it brought order. People rise and sleep under the blanket of time. They plan their days, weeks, years, and entire lives around its surety. People aboard the Empress were convinced that in a short time, they would be in England. Yet, time proved to be a paradox. The very thing that is considered trustworthy, is unpredictable. The reliance on time, on order, brings chaos when time pulls the floor out from under us.

Grace had read a report in the Toronto Globe telling of the background of the building of the Empress of Ireland. From the original sketch of the ship in November, 1904, to her launch on January 27, 1906, she had been designed and built by thousands of people employed by the CPR in Govan, Scotland. Thousands of hours and many years of accumulated craftsmanship experience were invested in her. It was expected that she would last a long time. Yet, all this investment of time was stripped away in only fourteen minutes. Time had undermined the plans of many.

Like Paden, Grace felt like she had been transformed forever. She recalled standing on the ship's hull as it was sinking. Was it the face of a young woman she had seen in the porthole? Or, was it her reflection? It disappeared, never to be seen again. Perhaps, it was as though a part of her had died on the Empress. She had been given a glimpse through the porthole of death. She had seen death up close, but was pulled back to life on this side of the glass. She would now live life in a different measure.

Once Paden had completely slipped out of view through the station doors, Grace turned to look across the street to one of the buildings, deep in Toronto's downtown. She noticed a window. It was emblazoned with a large cross. A red cross. She moved towards the cross with conviction, knowing that very soon, according to many reports, the world would be in a great war that would bring turmoil. She knew that she had to volunteer and assist in what ways she could. Her brush with death had shown her that she had been saved to serve suffering humanity.

*Salvationist victims are laid to rest
at Mount Pleasant Cemetery on June 6, 1914.*

From the Author

The fictional storyline of thievery and murder aboard the Empress of Ireland is not meant to put a blemish on the reputation of the ship's passengers and crew. Instead, it is intended to be a way of attracting people to the true historical account, one of brave suffering, sacrifice, and salvation.